YORK NOTES

KT-143-275

MACBETH

WILLIAM SHAKESPEARE

NOTES BY JAMES SALE

Longman
is an imprint of

PEARSON

York Press

The right of James Sale to be identified as Author of this Work has been asserted by him in accordance with the Copyright, Designs and Patents Act 1988

YORK PRESS
322 Old Brompton Road, London SW5 9JH

PEARSON EDUCATION LIMITED
Edinburgh Gate, Harlow,
Essex CM20 2JE, United Kingdom
Associated companies, branches and representatives throughout the world

© Librairie du Liban Publishers 1997, 2002, 2010

All rights reserved. No part of this publication may be reproduced, stored in a retrieval system, or transmitted in any form or by any means, electronic, mechanical, photocopying, recording, or otherwise, without either the prior written permission of the Publishers or a licence permitting restricted copying in the United Kingdom issued by the Copyright Licensing Agency Ltd, Saffron House, 6–10 Kirby Street, London EC1N 8TS

First published 1997
New edition 2002
This new and fully revised edition 2010

14 13 12
Imp 10 9 8 7 6 5

ISBN 978–1–4082–4879–9

Illustrations by Bob Moulder; and Neil Gower (p. 6 only)
Phototypeset by Pantek Arts Ltd, Maidstone
Printed in China (GCC/05)

CONTENTS

PART FOUR
KEY CONTEXT AND THEMES

PART FIVE
LANGUAGE AND STRUCTURE

PART SIX
GRADE BOOSTER

Study and revision advice

There are two main stages to your reading and work on *Macbeth*. Firstly, the study of the book as you read it. Secondly, your preparation or revision for examination or Controlled Assessment. These top tips will help you with both.

READING AND STUDYING THE PLAY — DEVELOP INDEPENDENCE!

- Try to engage and respond **personally** to the characters, themes and story – not just for your enjoyment, but also because it helps you develop your own, **independent ideas and thoughts** about *Macbeth*. This is something that examiners are very keen to see.

- **Talk** about the text with friends and family; ask questions in class; put forward your own viewpoint – and, if time, **read around** the text to find out about life in Shakespeare's day.

- Take time to **consider** and **reflect** about the **key elements** of the play; keep your own notes, mind-maps, diagrams, scribbled jottings about the characters and how you respond to them; follow the story as it progresses (what do you think might happen?); discuss the main themes and ideas (what do *you* think it is about? Ambition? Greed? Bravery?); pick out language that impresses you or makes an **impact**; and so on.

- Treat your studying **creatively**. When you write essays or give talks about the play make your responses creative. Think about using really clear ways of explaining yourself, use unusual quotations, well-chosen vocabulary, and try powerful, persuasive ways of beginning or ending what you say or write.

REVISION — DEVELOP ROUTINES AND PLANS!

- **Good revision** comes from **good planning**. Find out when your examination or Controlled Assessment is and then plan to look at key aspects of *Macbeth* on different days or times during your revision period. You could use these Notes – see **How can these Notes help me?** – and add dates or times when you are going to cover a particular topic.

- Use **different ways** of **revising**. Sometimes talking about the text and what you know/don't know with a friend or member of the family can help; other times, filling a sheet of A4 with all your ideas in different colour pens about a character, for example Lady Macbeth, can make ideas come alive; also, making short lists of quotations to learn, or numbering events in the plot can assist you.

- **Practise plans** and **essays**. As you get nearer the 'day', start by looking at essay **questions** and writing short bulleted plans. Do several plans [you don't have to write the whole essay]; then take those plans and add details to them [quotations, linked ideas]. Finally, using the advice in **Part Six: Grade Booster**, write some practice essays and then check them out against the advice we have provided.

> **EXAMINER'S TIP**
>
> Prepare for the examination/ assessment! Whatever you need to bring, make sure you have it with you – books, if you're allowed, pens, pencils – and that you turn up on time!

Introducing *Macbeth*

SETTING

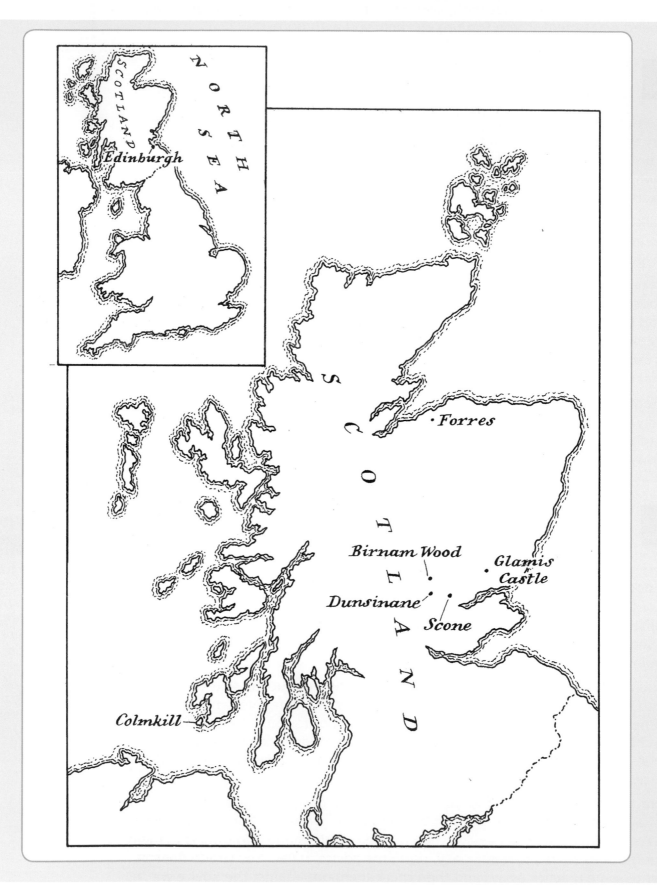

CHARACTERS: WHO'S WHO

Banquo, friend of Macbeth

Macbeth

Lady Macbeth

Duncan, King of Scotland

Macduff, Thane of Fife

Three witches

Malcolm. Duncan's son and heir to his throne.

WILLIAM SHAKESPEARE: AUTHOR AND CONTEXT

1558 Elizabeth I becomes Queen of England

1564 William Shakespeare is baptised on 26 April in Stratford-on-Avon, Warwickshire

1593–4 Outbreak of the Plague in London, closing theatres and killing as many as 5,000, according to some sources

1590–4 Shakespeare's early published works and poems written when theatres are closed by the Plague

1594 Joins Lord Chamberlain's Men (from 1603 named the King's Men) as actor and playwright

1599 Moves to newly opened Globe Theatre

1599–1608 Writes his greatest plays, including *Macbeth*, *King Lear* and *Hamlet*

1603 Elizabeth I dies on 24 March; James I (James VI of Scotland), son of Mary, succeeds to throne of England

1605 The Gunpowder Plot

1616 Shakespeare dies, 23 April, and is buried in Stratford

PART TWO: Plot and Action

Plot summary: What happens in *Macbeth*?

REVISION ACTIVITY

- Go through the summary boxes below and **highlight** what you think is the **key moment** in each Act.
- Then find each moment in the **text** and **reread** it. Write down **two reasons** why you think each moment is so **important**.

ACT I

- King Duncan plans to reward brave Macbeth with the title Thane of Cawdor for having defeated rebel forces in battle.

- Three witches inform Macbeth he will be Thane of Cawdor and King of Scotland.

- Macbeth is officially informed that he has become Thane of Cawdor. He is amazed the witches' prophecy has come true and reveals his hopes for the crown of Scotland.

- Macbeth's wife, Lady Macbeth, shares his ambition and calls on evil spirits to give her the strength to undertake the murder of Duncan.

- Duncan arrives at Macbeth's castle, where he is welcomed.

- When Macbeth arrives home his wife insists on planning the murder.

ACT II

- Worried about the murder he is about to commit, Macbeth sees a vision of a dagger.

- He murders Duncan, although afterwards Lady Macbeth criticises him for being distressed. She helps to cover up the murder and they then go to bed to pretend innocence.

- Macduff finds Duncan murdered and the alarm is sounded.

- Macbeth slays Duncan's guards to cover his crime, but says he did it in fury because they murdered Duncan.

- Duncan's sons, Malcolm and Donalbain, slip away in fear of their lives.

- Macbeth succeeds to the throne but Macduff will not attend Macbeth's coronation.

Act III

Banquo suspects Macbeth of treachery and Macbeth orders his murder and the murder of Banquo's son, Fleance. Although Banquo is killed, Fleance escapes.

Banquo's ghost appears at Macbeth's banquet and terrorises Macbeth, whose behaviour indicates his guilt to fellow guests.

Macbeth, now acting independently of his wife, plans to see the witches again.

The witches prepare to meet him.

Macduff flies to the English court, leaving his wife and children behind at his castle.

Act IV

- Macbeth visits the witches and discovers that he should fear Macduff, but that no man born of a woman can harm him. He also learns that he will never be beaten until Birnam Wood comes to Dunsinane.

- After leaving the witches, Macbeth orders the murder of Macduff's wife and children.

- In England, Malcolm tests the loyalty of Macduff, who has recently arrived there, fleeing from Scotland.

- Macduff learns of the slaughter of his entire family by Macbeth's soldiers.

- When Malcolm informs Macduff that England will provide an army under Siward to defeat Macbeth, Macduff vows personally to kill Macbeth.

Act V

- The English army marches on Macbeth disguised with branches. Macbeth fortifies his castle at Dunsinane and prepares for a long siege.

- Macbeth learns his wife has died – apparently by suicide – but he is unconcerned as his life appears to lack any meaning.

- He is enraged when a messenger tells him that Birnam Wood is coming to Dunsinane.

- He abandons his siege plan and goes out to fight; although his army is losing, nobody seems able to kill Macbeth himself. He meets Macduff, who was born by Caesarian (so not of woman), and Macduff kills Macbeth in single combat.

- Macduff hails Malcolm as King of Scotland and Malcolm invites all to attend his coronation at Scone.

Act I Scene 1: Meeting the witches

SUMMARY

❶ Shakespeare presents three witches meeting in the middle of a storm and preparing to entice Macbeth to evil.

❷ Their riddling rhymes show that they use supernatural powers.

WHY IS THIS SCENE IMPORTANT?

A It **immediately** grabs our **attention** by its dramatic non-realism.

B It raises our sense of **curiosity** and **expectancy**.

C It establishes the importance of **supernatural** powers in the play.

D It provides an initial clue about a key **theme** of **good** and **evil**.

CREATING CURIOSITY AND EXPECTANCY

The opening scene of the play is extremely brief, but this helps create a sense of mystery and wonder. Little is explained – a violent storm, three strange witch-like creatures speaking in rhyme, and waiting in an ominous way for Macbeth.

Shakespeare heightens this atmosphere by the first word: 'When' – a question. Others quickly follow. Who is Macbeth, we wonder? And why are they interested in him? The air is 'filthy' (line 12) and this also suggests dark deeds are about to happen – our imagination is captured.

THE WITCHES – GOOD OR EVIL?

The witches, as Shakespeare presents them, are ambiguous creatures – perhaps not even human. They are sometimes called the Weird Sisters. To form a full picture you will need to study their appearances in Act I Scene 3 and Act IV Scene 1.

The fact that they are evil is shown in their final **couplet**. This means: good is bad and bad is good. The witches are violating God's natural order.

EXAMINER'S TIP: WRITING ABOUT WITCHCRAFT

Remember that the best answers take the text seriously. The idea of witchcraft is still popular today, with lots of books and films made about the topic. In the 1600s it was much more common to think that witchcraft was real. Shakespeare and his patron, King James I, believed in witchcraft, and practising it was a crime punishable by death.

Focus on Shakespeare's idea that witchcraft turns the world upside down: fair is foul – its opposite; the battle is lost and won – its contradiction. Link this with other examples in the play of where Shakespeare gives the idea that what seems to be reality proves not to be. Especially consider Macbeth's words at the end of the play: 'be these juggling fiends no more believed / That palter with us in a double sense' (V. 8.19–20).

KEY QUOTE

'Fair is foul and foul is fair'

CHECKPOINT 1

How does Shakespeare show and interest us in the witches at the beginning of the play?

? DID YOU KNOW

Macbeth has traditionally been considered an 'unlucky' play. It is referred to as 'The Scottish Play' by the players.

GLOSSARY

palter evade or deceive

Act I Scene 2: Macbeth and Banquo's bravery

SUMMARY

① King Duncan receives news that the battle against the rebel Macdonwald was evenly balanced, but that Macbeth has beaten him.

② Reinforcements from the King of Norway attack Macbeth and Banquo.

③ Duncan hears that, through the courage of Macbeth, his army has won.

④ Duncan declares that the traitor Thane of Cawdor is to be executed and Macbeth is to receive his title and lands as a reward.

WHY IS THIS SCENE IMPORTANT?

A Shakespeare **interests** us further about **who Macbeth is**, as we learn about him by **report**.

B We switch from the **shadowy world** of **witches** to the **physical world** of **battle**.

C We discover that Macbeth and Banquo have displayed outstanding **bravery** in the fight.

D We learn that Duncan, the king, is **generous** and **kind**.

E We find out that Macbeth is to be made **Thane of Cawdor**.

> **KEY QUOTE**
>
> 'brave Macbeth (well he deserves that name)'

THE CHARACTER – WHO IS MACBETH?

Shakespeare has not yet shown us Macbeth. The witches mentioned him earlier. Now the Captain and Ross do. While the battle has been violent, their descriptions give it a heroic quality, especially Macbeth's part in it.

He is described as 'Valour's minion' (line 19) and 'Bellona's bridegroom' (line 55) – Bravery's favourite and the husband of War. Duncan himself praises Macbeth as 'valiant', a 'Worthy gentleman' (line 24) and as 'noble' (line 70).

MACBETH AND BANQUO – BRAVERY AS AN IMPORTANT QUALITY

Macbeth and Banquo are both presented as heroic warriors. Both remain brave throughout the play, although it may be argued that many of Macbeth's later actions are wicked and cowardly. Notice how appeals to courage always tempt Macbeth – for Macbeth bravery is the essence of being a man.

> **GRADE BOOSTER**
>
> Contrast the differences that Shakespeare shows us between Banquo and Macbeth – both are brave, but how different are their fates and reputations by the end of the play?

EXAMINER'S TIP: WRITING ABOUT IRONY

Understanding the concept of irony, and exploring how Shakespeare uses it in the play is important for attaining higher grades. The use of irony – more specifically, dramatic irony – is particularly important.

Shakespeare explores the subtle distinctions between what appears to be so and what actually is. A good example is Duncan's comment that he will not be deceived by the Thane of Cawdor any more (lines 66–7). The original Thane of Cawdor attempts to take the throne, and is executed. The new Thane of Cawdor – Macbeth – succeeds!

> **GLOSSARY**
>
> **Thane/thane** lord
>
> **valour's minion** the servant of courage

Act I Scene 3: The witches meet Macbeth and Banquo

SUMMARY

① Macbeth and Banquo meet the witches.

② They greet Macbeth and inform him that he will become Thane of Cawdor and King of Scotland.

③ Whilst Macbeth is stunned by these prophecies, Banquo demands they tell him of his future. He is told that although he will not be king, his offspring will be.

④ Messengers from Duncan inform Macbeth that he is now Thane of Cawdor.

⑤ Macbeth is astonished by the news; Banquo warns Macbeth of danger; Macbeth is preoccupied by thoughts of kingship, which he tries to hide.

WHY IS THIS SCENE IMPORTANT?

A We learn there is a **limit** to the witches' power.
B Shakespeare draws important **contrasts** between Banquo and Macbeth.
C The **theme** of **ambition** is introduced.

THE POWER OF THE WITCHES – AND ITS LIMITS

The scene begins with the witches boasting about evil deeds they have committed, but it reveals some limitations to their power. In their attack upon the 'master o' the *Tiger*' (line 8) they admit that they cannot make his ship sink (line 25).

What they do to him, however, hints at what will happen to Macbeth: they will 'drain him dry as hay' (line 19), he will be sleepless (lines 20–3) and he will 'dwindle, peak, and pine' (line 24).

MACBETH AND BANQUO – THEIR CONTRAST

Ross tells Macbeth he has become the Thane of Cawdor. Macbeth and Banquo are both amazed, and we begin to see Macbeth's ambition unfolding through the asides – or **soliloquys** – he delivers to the audience. Banquo warns of the danger of trusting such supernatural messages, but Macbeth is lost in his own thoughts, thinking through all the implications.

Banquo's description of the witches is important in seeing how unnatural they are: they seem to be women but are not. It is Banquo who thinks they are evil: 'What! Can the devil speak true?' (line 108). Macbeth does not. Note how keen Macbeth is to hear more of this 'strange intelligence' (line 77): 'Would they had stayed!' (line 83).

EXAMINER'S TIP: WRITING ABOUT IMAGERY

Shakespeare begins to develop the **imagery** of clothing – 'borrowed robes' (line 110) and 'strange garments' (line 146). This is significant because clothing is a powerful image suggesting concealment and disguise: Macbeth, as it were, hides behind his clothes of kingship. Look for this imagery in other, later references.

KEY QUOTE

'And oftentimes, to win us to our harm,
The instruments of darkness tell us truths'

CHECKPOINT 2

Why does Shakespeare have Macbeth wish the witches had stayed?

GRADE BOOSTER

The soliloquy beginning 'Two truths are told' (line 128) shows that Macbeth all too quickly begins imagining the steps he will need to take – that is, murdering Duncan – to become king. Notice how the real horror of doing the deed seems to be balanced by a morbid fascination at its prospect.

DID YOU KNOW

Many writers throughout history have composed their works for kings, queens or rich or important persons. This is called patronage.

Act I Scene 4: King Duncan names his son, Malcolm, his heir

SUMMARY

① King Duncan asks his son, Malcolm, about the execution of the Thane of Cawdor.

② He is told that Cawdor died repenting of his actions and with dignity.

③ Macbeth and Banquo arrive and are thanked by Duncan for their efforts.

④ Duncan announces that his son, Malcolm, is to be his heir and also that he will visit Macbeth in his castle at Inverness.

⑤ Macbeth leaves to prepare for the arrival of the king, but we learn that the announcement of Malcolm as heir is a bitter blow to him.

⑥ In Macbeth's absence, Duncan praises him to Banquo.

WHY IS THIS SCENE IMPORTANT?

A The announcement of Malcolm as heir provides Macbeth with **motivation** to prevent this happening by committing **murder** and **treason**.

B Shakespeare shows how Macbeth's **attitude** has **changed** and **hardened**.

C Shakespeare contrasts even further the difference between the **reality** of the situation and the **appearance**.

D Macbeth's character is **contrasted** with Duncan, Banquo and even the executed Thane of Cawdor.

CONTRASTING CHARACTERS – MACBETH, BANQUO, DUNCAN AND THE THANE OF CAWDOR

The scene highlights a series of further contrasts: between Duncan and Banquo (who are open and direct) and Macbeth, who, Shakespeare shows, prefers to hide his desires and intentions. Typically, for Duncan, stars shine (line 41), whereas for Macbeth they 'hide' so that darkness prevails (lines 50–1). We also hear of the former Thane of Cawdor's noble death; this contrasts with the living Thane of Cawdor's evil ambition.

Again, it is ironic that Duncan should comment about the former Thane of Cawdor that 'There's no art / To find the mind's construction in the face' (lines 11–12), since he so clearly fails to read what is in the new Thane of Cawdor's face. His trust of Macbeth leads to his death. Shakespeare's use of these contrasts serves to establish two contrary things: first, just how good and worthy a king Duncan is; second, just how appalling a crime it would be for Macbeth to murder him.

EXAMINER'S TIP: WRITING ABOUT SHAKESPEARE'S DEVELOPMENT OF CHARACTER

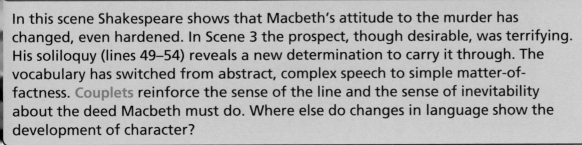

In this scene Shakespeare shows that Macbeth's attitude to the murder has changed, even hardened. In Scene 3 the prospect, though desirable, was terrifying. His soliloquy (lines 49–54) reveals a new determination to carry it through. The vocabulary has switched from abstract, complex speech to simple matter-of-factness. Couplets reinforce the sense of the line and the sense of inevitability about the deed Macbeth must do. Where else do changes in language show the development of character?

CHECKPOINT 3

How does the announcement of Malcolm as heir to the throne affect Macbeth?

? DID YOU KNOW

Malcolm reigned as Malcolm III and his son, Duncan, became Duncan II.

Act I Scene 5: Lady Macbeth is determined to be queen

SUMMARY

❶ Shakespeare presents Lady Macbeth reading a letter from her husband informing her of his success in battle and, more importantly, of his encounter with the witches.

❷ Macbeth believes their knowledge to be true, and communicates his excitement about his destiny to be king – and so for her to be queen.

❸ After reading the letter, she is worried that Macbeth is too soft a person to be able to take the crown. She is determined that she will assist him through 'the valour of my tongue' (line 26).

❹ On hearing – to her great surprise – that the king himself will be staying in their castle overnight, she is overjoyed and calls on demonic spirits to harden her own resolve and to destroy any weakness or pity.

❺ Macbeth enters and she immediately sets to work to convince him that he should murder Duncan.

❻ He says little but she insists that the deed must be done, that she will personally organise its operation, and finally that failure to accomplish this act would be a form of fear.

KEY QUOTE

'Thou wouldst be great – / Art not without ambition, but without / The illness should attend it'

WHY IS THIS SCENE IMPORTANT?

A Shakespeare establishes the **close relationship** between Macbeth and his wife.
B **Supernatural** forces are re-introduced by Lady Macbeth's calling on them.
C The scale and scope of the evil contemplated is heightened further by her **language**.
D We learn that Macbeth has 'human kindness' (line 16) in him that may resist the **temptation**.
E Shakespeare arouses our **curiosity** about what happens next.

THE FORCE OF LADY MACBETH'S CHARACTER

Lady Macbeth immediately understands what her husband's letter means. Her response is direct and to the point: her husband must be what he has been promised – king of Scotland. No fine points of conscience or loyalty seem to worry her, and it is noticeable how Shakespeare portrays her as overwhelming her husband when he appears. It is also interesting to reflect how she instantly taps into the spirit world: her 'spirits' (line 25, an interesting plural) will invade Macbeth's ear, and she literally does ask spirits to possess her body.

The point about her 'unsex'-ing (line 40) and her 'woman's breasts' (line 46) no longer being used for milk but for murder, shows a curious parallel with the ambiguous sexuality of the witches themselves. It is as if, at this level of evil, one abandons being either male or female – one is a neutral 'it'. Later (I.7.46), Macbeth himself, in trying to deflect his wife's arguments, puts forward the view that in daring/doing more than what is proper – or natural – for a man to do, one is no longer a man. Despite his argument, he, of course, does precisely that.

THE RELATIONSHIP BETWEEN MACBETH AND HIS WIFE

The letter to Lady Macbeth shows not only complete trust in his wife – for such a letter could itself be interpreted as treasonous – but also affection and love: 'my dearest partner of greatness' (line 10) suggests a warm equality. Later we will see how this affection cools.

EXAMINER'S TIP: WRITING ABOUT IMAGERY

We have already seen the bloody nature of battle in Scene 2. Shakespeare develops the imagery of blood throughout the play. Look at what Lady Macbeth requests: 'Make thick my blood' (line 42). Here blood is seen as a natural function of the human body, one that feeds the human capacity for compassion and repentance – things she wishes stopped. Technically, 'Make thick my blood' is a figure of speech called a metaphor. When writing about imagery, remember to look for different ways in which an image, such as blood, is used.

? DID YOU KNOW

Lady Macbeth's real name was Gruoch (pronounced GROO-och). She was the granddaughter of a murdered Scottish king. Macbeth was her second husband.

Act I Scene 6: Duncan arrives at Macbeth's castle

SUMMARY

❶ King Duncan arrives at Macbeth's castle with his sons and attendant thanes. He admires the air.

❷ Lady Macbeth – without her husband – greets Duncan and they exchange greetings and compliments. Duncan takes her hand and is led into the castle.

KEY QUOTE

'This castle hath a pleasant seat'

CHECKPOINT 4

Shakespeare shows appearances can be deceptive: where else is this very evident?

WHY IS THIS SCENE IMPORTANT?

A Shakespeare continues developing the **theme** of **appearances** (we are loyal to the king) versus reality (we are really going to murder him).

B Shakespeare shows **Lady Macbeth** fully **involved** in the **deception** and the **treachery**.

C Again, we contrast Duncan's **open** and **free** nature with that of the Macbeths.

APPEARANCE AND REALITY

Once more Shakespeare shows how reality and appearance are different. The air and the castle appear delightful, but are in reality to be the site of foul murder. In addition, although he is arriving at Macbeth's original 'home' of Glamis, he asks after him with his new title: 'Where's the Thane of Cawdor?' (line 20) – **ironically** reminding us of what the first Thane of Cawdor committed.

Lady Macbeth speaks of 'those honours deep and broad' (line 17) that Duncan has rewarded them with – while planning to murder him. Although she expresses appreciation for the honours, her heart, as Shakespeare demonstrates, is full of contempt, ingratitude and murder.

EXAMINER'S TIP: WRITING ABOUT DUNCAN

Although this is the last scene in which he appears in person, it's important to remember that Duncan is a major character. This is because his influence pervades the play and he sets the standard for what a king should be. Even Macbeth admires him – he describes him as 'gracious' (III.1.65) after he has murdered him – and Macduff refers to him as 'a most sainted King' (IV.3.109). This means that the view of Duncan is consistent throughout the play (unlike views of Macbeth).

Duncan is honest, sincere and above all, honourable. There is a warmth about Duncan – he seems to enjoy the achievements of others and his gifts are not given to gain his own advantage. It is horribly ironic that our final view of Duncan is of him kissing his hostess Lady Macbeth, and we later learn that he has sent her a diamond as a present (Act II Scene 1).

GRADE BOOSTER

When writing about Duncan, you could think about whether he has any weaknesses as a character in spite of all his good qualities. Is it a weakness to be so trusting as a king?

Act I Scene 7: Macbeth debates whether to murder Duncan

SUMMARY

- Macbeth, alone, debates in his own mind the pros and cons of murdering Duncan.

- He worries that murdering his own lord and guest would set an example that would return to plague him. Also, Duncan has been such a good king, heaven itself will expose the wickedness of Macbeth.

- The only justification for the murder is, finally, his ambition.

- However, his own imagery of damnation frightens him and he resolves not to go ahead with the murder.

- His wife enters and he informs her he has changed his mind and will not murder Duncan – why should he throw away all the glory he has so recently gained?

- She is contemptuous of his change of heart and accuses him of cowardice. They argue but her violent determination wins – she outlines the plan – and he agrees to it.

WHY IS THIS SCENE IMPORTANT?

A Shakespeare graphically shows a man **wrestling** with his own **conscience** – the choice of evil was not inevitable or even easy for Macbeth.

B One major theme of the play – Macbeth's **ambition** – is stated overtly in this scene.

C Shakespeare portrays Macbeth's **vulnerability** to accusations of cowardice and lack of manliness.

D Lady Macbeth establishes her full share of **responsibility** for what is to unfold.

E The idea that *one* murder will be sufficient – Macbeth's earlier hope – is already (ironically) **undermined** in Lady Macbeth's immediate **plan** to implicate the guards.

MACBETH'S FATAL WEAKNESS

Lady Macbeth attacks her husband exactly where she knows it will hurt: his courage and manhood are at stake. And she does what she said she would do in Act I Scene 5, 'pour my spirits in thine ear' (I.5.25). Shakespeare demonstrates her strength of purpose and her leadership, which offer a remarkable contrast to Macbeth's performance at this stage.

Later, once king, Macbeth himself will appeal to Banquo's murderers in exactly the same way: if they are 'men' they will commit murder (III.1.91–107). At the end of the play, his courage and manhood are all that is left of him; so he fights Macduff knowing that he is doomed.

LADY MACBETH'S DEADLY PERSUASIVENESS

This is the critical scene in which all the arguments against treason and murder are explicitly and strongly made. Lady Macbeth demolishes them all by questioning her husband's manhood. Macbeth almost concedes that his wife is more manly than he is: her 'undaunted mettle should compose / Nothing but males' (lines 73–4). Thus, he falls into her way of thinking. Notice how Shakespeare uses his final words in this scene, 'False face must hide what the false heart doth know' (line 82), to echo Lady Macbeth's earlier advice (I.5.61–4).

> **? DID YOU KNOW**
>
> Historically, Banquo assisted Macbeth in killing Duncan!

> **KEY QUOTE**
>
> 'I have no spur / To prick the sides of my intent, but only / Vaulting ambition'

> **GLOSSARY**
>
> mettle spirit of courage

Act II Scene 1: Macbeth and Banquo meet briefly

SUMMARY

❶ On his way to bed, Banquo has a premonition something is wrong, and then encounters Macbeth.

❷ He presents him with a diamond for Macbeth's wife, a gift from the king.

❸ Banquo tells Macbeth that he dreamt of the witches. Macbeth dismisses thoughts of them, but requests that he and Banquo speak about the matter another time.

❹ Banquo agrees but not without the reservation that honour should not be compromised.

❺ Macbeth is left alone and imagines he sees a dagger in front of him – a dagger which guides him towards his goal of killing Duncan.

❻ As the bell rings, he determines to go ahead and murder the king.

WHY IS THIS SCENE IMPORTANT?

A Shakespeare **intensifies** the **atmosphere** of night and evil.

B The **contrast** of Macbeth's thoughts with Banquo's **integrity** is clear.

C Shakespeare shows us the **effect** of the witches on Banquo, as he struggles against the evil.

D Further honours from the king highlight Macbeth's **disloyalty** even more.

E Macbeth's struggle with his **conscience** is decisively resolved.

F Shakespeare leaves us in great **tension**, anticipating what comes next.

MACBETH AND BANQUO FURTHER CONTRASTED

Shakepeare's introduction of Banquo at this point allows us another point of contrast with Macbeth. We see the witches have affected him too – but whereas Macbeth has surrendered his will to them, only Banquo's dreams are invaded.

Macbeth's request to talk of the witches later with its promise to 'make honour for you' (line 26) is an attempt to sound Banquo out – how will he react should Macbeth become king? Banquo's answer, which insists upon maintaining integrity, is hardly likely to please Macbeth. Shakespeare shows Banquo cannot be bought. It is not surprising that later Shakespeare has Macbeth comment that he feels 'rebuked' (III.1.55) by Banquo.

EXAMINER'S TIP: WRITING ABOUT ATMOSPHERE

Notice how Shakespeare depicts the scene as dark – torches are necessary to light the way. Banquo senses something is wrong. He notes that the stars' 'candles are all out' (line 5) – a metaphor suggesting that the physical darkness is also a moral darkness. He uses a simile to describe the effect on him: 'A heavy summons lies like lead upon me' (line 6).

Later, when Macbeth is on his own, he does see something in the dark, not a star, but a dagger. Is this a real dagger or a 'false creation / Proceeding from the heat-oppressèd brain' (lines 39–40)? The witches were real enough, but now Macbeth has embarked on evil he begins to see things that others cannot. Shakespeare shows these images terrifying him, and this intensifies the atmosphere of evil.

KEY QUOTE

'Thou marshall'st me the way that I was going – / And such an instrument I was to use.'

? DID YOU KNOW

Macbeth is one of Shakespeare's shortest plays (only *The Comedy of Errors* and *The Tempest* are shorter) and one reason is because there is no subplot.

CHECKPOINT 5

How does Shakespeare portray Banquo as appearing more open than Macbeth?

Act II Scene 2: Macbeth murders King Duncan

SUMMARY

1 Nerves on edge, Lady Macbeth waits for Macbeth to return from having committed the murder. Her mood is bold, and she boasts how she has drugged the guards.

2 Macbeth enters, carrying two bloodstained daggers. He is obsessed by the noises he has heard.

3 The guilt of what he has done torments him, and Lady Macbeth attempts to lessen and rationalise his fears.

4 She then criticises him for failing to leave the daggers on the guards, and has to go back herself and plant the weapons on them – Macbeth is too frightened.

5 A knocking at the gate means they must quickly go to bed and pretend to be surprised when Duncan's body is discovered.

WHY IS THIS SCENE IMPORTANT?

A Up till this point Macbeth had options – now there is **no going back**.

B Shakespeare demonstrates the scale of the terrifying **guilt** in that a great warrior like Macbeth is reduced to abject fear.

C Lady Macbeth's character, by contrast, is shown by Shakespeare as **steely** and **determined** – where Macbeth **flounders**, Lady Macbeth **perseveres**.

LADY MACBETH'S RESOLVE

Despite some nervous worry early on, Lady Macbeth is entirely in control of herself and of her husband. She planned the execution, and now it is her readiness of mind and strength of purpose that compensate for Macbeth's failure to act decisively once the murder is committed.

Shakespeare shows Lady Macbeth focused on the need to keep to the plan of action – ordering Macbeth to go back and place the daggers beside the guards, so as to incriminate them. Macbeth, however, is too terrified to return. He is much more concerned with the spiritual and moral implications of what he has done: the deep damnation, in fact, that he has brought upon himself.

EXAMINER'S TIP: WRITING ABOUT THE LANGUAGE OF THE PLAY

In Macbeth's 'Will all great Neptune's ocean' (lines 57–60) speech, Shakespeare expands the language into the grandiose 'multitudinous seas incarnadine', and then just as suddenly deflates it into the simple 'green one, red'. Through the 'posh' vocabulary Shakespeare enables Macbeth to cloud what he has done; but the simple vocabulary returns him (and us) to the truth – he has spilled innocent blood. Look for other places where the kind of language used gives us insights into a character or situation.

KEY CONNECTIONS

The murder of Duncan is not physically shown on stage in the text of the play. However, it is included in the 1971 Roman Polanski film version of *Macbeth*.

KEY QUOTE

'Macbeth shall sleep no more!'

★ GRADE BOOSTER

Think creatively about Shakespeare's language. For example, the need for an 'Amen' (line 29), which Macbeth cannot speak, and the fact that even the ocean cannot clean him (lines 57–60), suggest that there is little hope for Macbeth.

GLOSSARY

Neptune god of the sea
multitudinous having many elements or forms
incarnadine dye red

Act II Scene 3: The murder of Duncan is discovered

SUMMARY

❶ The knocking continues and the Porter, who feels unwell, goes to open the gate. He imagines he is the porter of hell. He lets in Macduff and Lennox.

❷ Seemingly awoken by their knocking, Macbeth comes forward to greet them. Macduff asks to be led to the king.

❸ Macduff, discovering the murder, returns, loudly proclaiming treason. As Macduff proceeds to stir the castle, Macbeth and Lennox rush in to ascertain the facts for themselves.

❹ Lady Macbeth appears, then Banquo, and both are informed of the reason for the commotion.

❺ Macbeth returns and bemoans the dreadful deed. Lennox suggests the guards may have been responsible, and it emerges that Macbeth immediately killed them.

❻ Macduff questions this, and as Macbeth justifies his actions, his wife faints, which distracts attention.

❼ Banquo assumes command and directs them to meet in readiness. Malcolm and Donalbain remain: they decide to flee, suspecting treachery from someone closely related.

> **CHECKPOINT 6**
>
> Why does Macbeth kill the guards?

WHY IS THIS SCENE IMPORTANT?

A Shakespeare **anticipates** the horror of Macbeth's reign: the 'hell' the Porter mentions (lines 1, 17) becomes a **reality**. Deception, murder, distrust, fear and flight are everywhere.

B Since we already know that the murder has been committed, this **delay** in its discovery heightens the tension and our sense of **anticipation**.

C Murder and deception lead to more murder and deception, as the themes are developed: the innocent guards are murdered to cover up the first crime.

D The escape of Malcolm and Donalbain provides **justification** for Macbeth's coronation while simultaneously meaning that he wears the crown uneasily, knowing they are alive and plotting against him. He will 'sleep no more' (II.2.40).

THE ROLE OF THE PORTER

The bleak intensity of the previous scene gives way to a brief comic interlude. Although the Porter is crude and rough, and his introduction by Shakespeare is intended to make us laugh, his role also performs other important functions. The continuation of physical knocking reminds us that we are still in the world where the Macbeths commit murder.

Earlier we have seen references to a 'serpent' (I.5.65) and a 'chalice' (I.7.11) and with that the suggestion that the Devil has entered into Macbeth. Later, Macduff is to say that Macbeth is a 'devil' (IV.3.56). Literally, then, Shakespeare would seem to suggest there is a hell where Macbeth is.

EXAMINER'S TIP: WRITING ABOUT HISTORICAL CONTEXT

It is useful to be able to talk about the historical context behind moments in the play. Interestingly, many of the Porter's speeches are connected to contemporary events: namely, the treasonous Gunpowder Plot. Thus, while making some good-humoured jokes, the overall thrust of the Porter's remarks is to widen the application of the play – hell is not only on the stage in Macbeth's castle, but present in the society for which Shakespeare was writing.

The Gunpowder Plot of 1605 was sensational in a number of ways: the sheer audacity of trying to blow up Parliament amazed the country, as did the scale of the treachery involved.

Shakespeare picks up this **theme** in the play: Banquo talks of the 'truths' which betray us (I.3.125), and the Porter debates the man who 'could not equivocate to heaven' (II.3.10–11). This is related to the wider theme of appearances. It was Lady Macbeth who advises Macbeth to 'look like the innocent flower / But be the serpent under't' (I.5.64–5).

KEY QUOTE

'There's daggers in men's smiles: the near in blood, The nearer bloody.'

GLOSSARY

equivocate in this sense, be economical with the truth

Act II Scene 4: Macbeth is named king

SUMMARY

① Ross and an old man recall the dreadful night of the murder.

② Macduff enters and tells them that Duncan's two sons are suspected of paying the guards to commit the murder, because they have now fled.

③ Macbeth has been nominated king and has gone to Scone to be crowned.

④ Ross asks Macduff whether he will go to the crowning. Macduff says he will not, but will return home to Fife.

⑤ Ross himself intends to go.

WHY IS THIS SCENE IMPORTANT?

A Shakespeare uses this scene to give us a **breathing space** before we meet the new king, Macbeth; further, it acts as a **commentary** on all that has happened.

B The old man is important because he is a **representative** of the people, and one whose **memory** goes back a long way – the crimes committed are without **parallel**.

C Shakespeare uses the extent of the **darkness** to symbolically remind us of Christ's crucifixion and the great darkness that the Bible says enveloped the land.

D We learn of Macduff's **suspicions** concerning Macbeth: he observes that the murderers were 'Those that Macbeth hath slain' (line 23) – and so could not be questioned – and that he will not go to Scone for the coronation.

E Shakespeare **contrasts** Macduff's attitude with Ross's readiness to go and to align himself with the new regime.

F Shakespeare's use of imagery explicitly reminds us of how the **natural order** has been turned upside down: a falcon killed by a 'mousing owl' (line 13) is an **unnatural** event.

SHAKESPEARE'S USE OF NARRATIVE PACE

Shakespeare has made Act II action packed! It is, after all, the culmination of the temptation of Macbeth. Act I has been about Macbeth's desire for kingship, and his succumbing to the temptation of achieving the throne via treachery and murder. Act II delivers his treachery and murder: in Scene 1 we see Macbeth following the dagger; in Scene 2 we hear the two conspirators after the murder is done, and Macbeth in abject fear and terror; in Scene 3 the Porter almost literally opens hell's gate and the murdered body is discovered, causing frantic commotion.

Now in Scene 4 Shakespeare allows us to pause, to reflect on the actions and events, yet at the same time provides further insights into the characters. In small, clever touches Shakespeare paints an essential difference between Ross and Macduff. In addition he introduces a minor character – an old man – who through his anonymity provides an unbiased commentary on the unnatural events that have occurred. In this way Shakespeare prepares us for the next round of monstrous murders that Macbeth will initiate.

CHECKPOINT 7

How important to the play is the character of Duncan?

DID YOU KNOW

Diana Wynyard, playing Lady Macbeth in 1948, said she did not believe in the play's bad luck. On the first night of her performance she slipped from the rostrum and fell fifteen feet!

KEY QUOTE

'A falcon, towering in her pride of place, Was by a mousing owl hawked at and killed.'

Act III Scene 1: Macbeth prepares his first murder as king

SUMMARY

❶ Banquo, alone, reflects on the witches' prophecies, and suspects that Macbeth did indeed obtain the crown through treachery.

❷ Macbeth and Lady Macbeth arrive.

❸ Macbeth pretends that he needs Banquo's advice on the following day on how to deal with Malcolm and Donalbain, who are abroad and spreading rumours.

❹ He learns from Banquo details of his journey and that Fleance will be with him.

❺ Macbeth then dismisses everyone. Alone, Macbeth reveals that he fears Banquo, and that the thought that Banquo's offspring should become kings is entirely unacceptable to him.

❻ Two murderers whom he wishes to see are brought in. To them he passionately outlines why Banquo is their mutual enemy, and they agree to perform the murder.

WHY IS THIS SCENE IMPORTANT?

A Shakespeare shows us more about the character of **Banquo**: Banquo leans more towards the prophecies without becoming, as Macbeth does, obsessed by them. From Macbeth's comments Banquo's **courage**, **wisdom** and **integrity** emerge.

B In the **first scene** in which Macbeth appears as **king**, Shakespeare reveals the kind of king he is and is going to be: entirely **treacherous**. Pretending to honour and value his former comrade-in-arms, he casually works out his movements to **entrap** and **murder** him and his son.

C Appropriately, Shakespeare shows Macbeth now **tempting** others to commit crimes with the same key argument with which he himself was tempted: namely, manhood – if you were a man, you would do it.

D **Lady Macbeth** is **not** part of this **plot**.

THE FALLEN NATURE OF MACBETH

Shakespeare demonstrates the depths to which Macbeth has sunk in his conversation with the murderers: here is a great warrior-hero who now has to meet the most vicious and corrupt kind of men in secret in order to both disguise and achieve his ends. The fact that he himself despises these men is shown in the way he addresses them – the interruption of the first murderer's solemn declaration of loyalty with the ironic 'Your spirits shine through you' (line 127) suggests contempt.

Subsequently, the mission of the third murderer (Act III Scene 3) shows how little he actually trusts the first two. But, then, trust is no longer something Macbeth believes in. Crucially, in the next scene (Act III Scene 2), even Lady Macbeth is not involved in his plans.

GRADE BOOSTER

Sometimes characters, like people, are contradictory! Think about how on the one hand, Macbeth believes the prophecies must come true, and on the other, he seeks to prevent them happening!

CHECKPOINT 8

Why is Lady Macbeth not involved in Macbeth's plan to kill Banquo?

KEY QUOTE

'come, Fate, into the list,
And champion me to the utterance!'

Act III Scene 2: Macbeth will commit another crime

SUMMARY

❶ Lady Macbeth wants to speak to her husband before the feast. She is not happy – uncertainty and insecurity trouble them both.

❷ Macbeth appears and she scolds him both for staying alone and for his continual dwelling on the actions they have done.

❸ Macbeth envies the peaceful dead. Lady Macbeth attempts to cheer him up.

❹ They discuss the feast ahead, resolve to praise Banquo at it, and then Macbeth reveals his fear of Banquo and Fleance.

❺ He then further reveals that he intends to commit another dreadful crime. He will not tell her what it is, but asks her to praise it when it's achieved.

❻ Lady Macbeth is amazed but drawn along with him.

? DID YOU KNOW

The Divine Right of Kings meant that because God appointed the king, he was not answerable to the people or to Parliament.

WHY IS THIS SCENE IMPORTANT?

A   We see Macbeth growing in evil, and **hardening himself** to commit **more crimes**.

B   Duncan's peace of mind – being dead – is now a source of **envy** to Macbeth, who is in torment and has dreadful **nightmares**.

C   Lady Macbeth is **no longer** controlling and driving the action of her husband.

D   The initial **hope** that they could enjoy their reign together is now exposed as **hollow**.

KEY QUOTE

'Things bad begun make strong themselves by ill!'

THE DEVELOPMENT OF EVIL

Shakespeare portrays Macbeth in an incubation period in which he grows stronger, and hardens himself to doing evil; for Lady Macbeth it is the start of her breakdown – she will take control one more time, at the banquet (Act III Scene 4), and then she will be overwhelmed by remorse for the tide of evil she has helped unleash, and go mad. Their roles are reversing.

In the encounters so far, Lady Macbeth has been dominant. Now Shakespeare shows the situation changing. Macbeth is keeping himself to himself and brooding on the crimes committed, and on the crimes he intends to commit – notice the bestial **imagery** again: 'O, full of scorpions is my mind' (line 36). Furthermore, he is not sharing his thoughts with his wife (in contrast to I.5.9–10) and so she is feeling isolated. This is despite the affectionate term – 'dearest chuck' (line 45) – Macbeth uses for her.

Act III Scene 3: Murderers kill Banquo

SUMMARY

❶ The two murderers are joined by a third.

❷ They wait for Banquo and Fleance, spring out and manage to kill Banquo.

❸ In the confusion Fleance escapes.

❹ The murderers resolve to inform Macbeth of what has been done.

WHY IS THIS SCENE IMPORTANT?

A We see that, despite the precaution of adding a third murderer, Fleance **escapes** – the witches' prophecy is not easily avoided for all Macbeth might do.

B The need to recruit a third murderer also indicates Macbeth's **distrust** of his first two.

C Whereas we **did not see** the actual murder of Duncan, but felt its horror, here Shakespeare enables us to **witness** what is to become routine assassination.

THE MURKY WORLD OF MACBETH

The addition of a third murderer adds nothing to the progress of the plot, but through it Shakespeare exposes the kind of world Macbeth inhabits and creates all around him. Macbeth trusts no one, not even the accomplices he has commissioned.

In the next scene (Act III Scene 4) we learn he has spies everywhere – everyone is being checked. Notice the night and day contrasts which Shakespeare draws through the play. The loss of light foreshadows the loss of life. Later on, Lady Macbeth will describe hell as 'murky' (V.1.32) – darkness has become Macbeth's preferred habitat.

EXAMINER'S TIP: WRITING ABOUT USE OF IMAGERY

It is worth noting Shakespeare's use of bestial imagery: how men can be classified in the same way as dogs. We remember that before he 'fell', Macbeth said he dared do all that a man should do – to do more was to be no man (I.7.46–7). In other words, acting like an animal is a natural consequence of his choices – and the imagery demonstrates that.

The bestial imagery also points to another factor in the degradation of Macbeth – animals cannot reason, and so have no choices. They act automatically on impulse. This lack of choice is something Macbeth comments on later when he observes, 'I am in blood / Stepped in so far, that, should I wade no more, / Returning were as tedious as go o'er' (III.4.136–8).

? DID YOU KNOW

The identity of the third murderer has caused much debate. Some have even suggested it is Macbeth in disguise! In the Polanski film version of the play Ross is depicted as the third murderer.

KEY QUOTE

'He needs not our mistrust'

Act III Scene 4: The murdered Banquo's ghost appears at the feast

SUMMARY

1 Macbeth welcomes various guests to his banquet.

2 The first murderer appears and Macbeth steps aside to speak with him. He learns that Banquo is dead, but that Fleance escaped – this disturbs him.

3 He returns to the feast and is gently reprimanded by his wife for his absence.

4 As he stands, making a speech praising Banquo, Banquo's ghost takes the only remaining chair.

5 Only Macbeth can see the ghost and he is terrified – only Lady Macbeth's quick thinking covers up the fact that Macbeth is beginning to reveal his guilt.

6 The ghost disappears and Macbeth regains his composure. Once more he tries to seem cheerful and praises the name of Banquo: the ghost reappears and Macbeth loses his nerve altogether.

7 He recovers himself when the ghost disappears again, but too late to enable the banquet to continue. Lady Macbeth heads off a question from Ross and dismisses everyone.

8 Alone with his wife, Macbeth confides that Macduff seems to be standing against him. He reveals, too, that he has spies everywhere, and that he intends to revisit the witches.

KEY QUOTE

'For mine own good / All causes shall give way.'

WHY IS THIS SCENE IMPORTANT?

A Shakespeare shows the Macbeths at the **high point** of their careers – on their thrones, entertaining their subjects, all of whom (except Macduff) are prepared to accept them.

B It ironically foreshadows the future: Banquo's ghost occupies Macbeth's seat, as his descendants will occupy his throne – and 'push us from our stools' (line 82).

C It marks the **beginning** of the **decline** of Macbeth's rule and power: he cannot keep calm on this important occasion of state, and almost reveals his **guilt**.

D The **supernatural** theme is re-introduced.

E It brilliantly exploits **dramatic tension**: the murdered man appearing at a State banquet – will he be seen? Macbeth almost blurting out the truth of his guilt – will he be exposed?

F We see that the **close bond** between Lady Macbeth and Macbeth is beginning to **dissolve**: she covers for him, but it is a dreadful strain on her, and he afterwards no longer talks of 'we' but of himself.

G Shakespeare has **structured** the play so that this is the **middle point**: Act I is about plans against King Duncan, Act II show actions against King Duncan, Act III is the reign of Macbeth before ... Act IV, where plans against King Macbeth start, and finally, to complete the structure, Shakespeare shows the actions against King Macbeth in Act V.

CONTRASTING MACBETH AND LADY MACBETH

The strain on Lady Macbeth is evident. Although he has been terrified, Macbeth, by the end of the scene, seems casual in his attitude to what has happened. His comment, 'We are yet but young in deed' (line 144) suggests that this mere blip will soon pass. She, however, as Shakespeare shows, has had to use all her resources and wit to contain the potential damage of exposure.

Earlier she had said 'Nought's had, all's spent' (III.2.4) and we see this particularly in this scene: she wanted to be queen and the scene begins with her keeping 'her state' (line 5), in other words, remaining on her throne. If there was anywhere in the play where Lady Macbeth could enjoy being queen to the full, it is here: on her throne, surrounded by subjects. Yet this, through Macbeth's actions, becomes a hollow and empty event, lacking any dignity or regal significance.

CHECKPOINT 9

What do you think the thanes would be thinking after the banquet?

EXAMINER'S TIP: WRITING ABOUT WITCHCRAFT AND PSYCHOLOGY

This scene raises the interesting question of witchcraft and psychology. Certainly, the supernatural motif is superbly developed by Shakespeare: we have had the witches, their prophecies, the dagger that led Macbeth to Duncan, and now we have the ghost of Banquo. But whereas Banquo saw and heard the witches alongside Macbeth, here only Macbeth sees the vision. As Lady Macbeth says, 'When all's done, / You look but on a stool' (lines 67–8).

This has practical implications for any production of the play – is the ghost just in Macbeth's mind (and so is not shown on stage), or does a ghost really appear? Perhaps because of its sheer dramatic impact, most versions of the play tend to want to include it. Think about what you would do if you were staging *Macbeth*.

CHECKPOINT 10

How is security Macbeth's 'chiefest enemy' (line 33)?

Act III Scene 5: The witches prepare to meet Macbeth again

SUMMARY

① The three witches and the goddess of witchcraft, Hecate, prepare a strong spell for deluding Macbeth.

WHY IS THIS SCENE IMPORTANT?

A Shakespeare introduces the idea of **layers of evil** – new depths, therefore, which Macbeth can sink to.

B As Macbeth in the preceding scene prepares to go to meet the witches, we learn they prepare to meet him – this rouses our **curiosity** and sense of **expectation**.

C Macbeth is described as a 'wayward son' (line 11) – so Shakespeare links Macbeth more organically to the **witches**, and we learn he has become fully **evil in nature**.

MACBETH AND EVIL

The witches' suggestion that Macbeth is a 'son' (line 11), although 'wayward', enables Shakespeare to indicate that Macbeth is no longer a victim of the witches' evil, but more a master – one of them – in their art. However, there can be no doubt – master or not – that by the end of the play he has so fully embraced evil, he has destroyed himself.

EXAMINER'S TIP: WRITING ABOUT EVIL

Nowadays, the word 'evil' is not much used, except in very extreme cases. People often refer to bad actions as 'unacceptable' rather than evil. The reference to 'security' being an enemy of human beings (lines 32–3) goes back to medieval Morality plays – it is how Satan, the devil, tempts mankind by playing on their fears of future loss. In the world of *Macbeth*, evil is an absolute that leads to a literal hell – as Macbeth himself is only too aware. Mentioning the historical context of the play can often improve your essay.

? **DID YOU KNOW**

The word 'weird' originally meant 'destiny' or 'fate'. The three Weird Sisters remind us of the three Fates of Greek mythology (Clotho, Lachesis and Atropo).

KEY QUOTE

'And you all know, security Is mortals' chiefest enemy.'

Act III Scene 6: The political situation in Scotland

SUMMARY

▶ Lennox outlines to another lord in deeply ironic terms his understanding of what has been happening in Scotland: that is, that Macbeth is responsible for all the murders that have plagued the state.

▶ Malcolm is in the English court attempting to raise military support to reclaim his throne. Lennox supports this.

▶ Macduff is in disgrace for refusing to attend Macbeth's banquet and is attempting to join Malcolm.

WHY IS THIS SCENE IMPORTANT?

A It shows the **direct consequence** of Macbeth's failure to control himself at his banquet: his lords have turned against him.

B It reveals that Macduff kept his **integrity** and went to Fife, not Macbeth's coronation.

C It outlines further the deficiencies in Macbeth's running of the state: not only the murders committed, but the **lack of fairness** and **honour** – in short, the **corruption** that blights everybody's life.

D We learn of **hope** in England, of Malcolm's welcome, and of another kind of king – 'the most pious Edward' (line 27) – whom Shakespeare provides as another **contrast** with Macbeth.

KEY QUOTE

'we may again Give to our tables meat, sleep to our nights, Free from our feasts and banquets bloody knives, Do faithful homage and receive free honours – All which we pine for now.'

MACBETH AND MACDUFF

Macbeth earlier had said he intended to 'send' for Macduff (III.4.129) and this scene briefly covers the fact that he has – Macduff has simply refused point-blank to attend. As Banquo is no longer a threat to Macbeth, Shakespeare provides another enemy, Macduff, who is moving centre stage to be the one to challenge Macbeth's power.

Banquo criticised the three witches, whose authority had impressed Macbeth; and it was Macduff who first queried Macbeth's behaviour with 'Wherefore did you so?' (II.3.103) when Macbeth revealed he had killed the guards. Shakespeare shows that Macbeth bitterly resents people with independent thought and ideas – and feels, in fact, that they must be got rid of.

Act IV Scene 1: The witches prophesy three things to Macbeth

Summary

1. Three witches create a powerful spell and prepare to meet Macbeth. Hecate joins them and approves their spell.

2. Macbeth then enters and commands them to answer his questions.

3. They call up powerful spirits to respond to him.

4. He is told three prophecies: that he should fear Macduff, that he cannot be harmed by one born of a woman and that he is secure until Birnam Wood comes to Dunsinane.

5. He then presses them for more information about Banquo's offspring and is mortified to see a vision of eight kings all descended from Banquo, who also appears.

6. The witches suddenly vanish and Macbeth curses them. Lennox appears and informs Macbeth that Macduff has fled to England.

7. Macbeth determines to kill Macduff's wife and children as a reprisal.

Why is this scene important?

KEY QUOTE

'Then live, Macduff. What need I fear of thee?
But yet I'll make assurance double sure,
And take a bond of fate'

A The spells show fully how **unnatural** the three witches are – the level of detail is revolting, and Shakespeare deliberately makes it so.

B Shakespeare portrays Macbeth's **complete confidence** in committing evil – he now dictates to the witches and threatens the 'masters'.

C As Macbeth commits to evil, so Macduff flies from Scotland in order to **challenge** him. Shakespeare creates **dramatic tension** by showing Macduff escaping at the point Macbeth is in pursuit.

D The irony of the **prophecies** intensifies: more are given, but they are double-edged. This is a **brilliant device** by Shakespeare because we want to learn how this will work out.

Macbeth and the agents of evil

Prior to his arrival, Macbeth is described as 'Something wicked' (line 45) – not even some*one*. Macbeth is one of their kind now. This is in line with the overall effect of evil in dehumanising the personality – the bestial imagery commented upon is also an example of this. So is the fact that they do a 'deed without a name' (line 49).

Shakespeare shows that earlier uncertainties have been stripped away. Before, the witches informed Macbeth of the prophecies; now he demands of them what he wants to know. He even threatens the powerful master spirits with a curse if they do not answer him (lines 104–5). When he leaves, there is no more agonising about what he needs to do – or discussing the situation with his wife – Macduff's castle is to be attacked. An extra point is the depths to which Macbeth has fallen in murdering, without any pity, women and children.

CHECKPOINT 11

How does Shakespeare heighten the sense of evil in this scene?

THE THEME OF SECURITY

Macbeth has been obsessed with the need for security since assassinating Duncan. For all his bravery, Shakespeare portrays him as frightened of what he cannot control. Hence his need to visit the witches and find the certainty of 'security' (III.5.32). One factor in establishing the trustworthiness of the prophecies in Macbeth's mind is the speed with which they happen: he became 'Cawdor' (I.3.106) immediately after the witches said he would; now, having been told to watch out for Macduff, Shakespeare has Lennox appear with the same warning.

EXAMINER'S TIP: WRITING ABOUT IRONY

Irony is central to the play. Here, the irony is that all the prophecies are double-edged and turn against him. Banquo's earlier comment accurately reflects the truth: 'The instruments of darkness tell us truths, / Win us with honest trifles, to betray's / In deepest consequence' (I.3.125–7). These words are prophetic and a condemnation of all that Macbeth comes to believe. Shakespeare has Banquo return – although dead – once more in this scene (with his eight heirs) to mock the stability of Macbeth's throne. Remember, when you are quoting from the play, that sometimes the words mean more than (sometimes even the opposite of) what they say.

Act IV Scene 2: Lady Macduff and her son are murdered

SUMMARY

❶ Lady Macduff is with her son and Ross. Ross informs her that her husband has fled to England. Lady Macduff accuses her husband of cowardice. Ross makes his excuses and leaves.

❷ A messenger arrives, warns of danger, and leaves. Murderers enter, kill Macduff's son, and pursue Lady Macduff with the same purpose.

KEY QUOTE

'I am in this earthly world, where to do harm Is often laudable, to do good sometime Accounted dangerous folly'

WHY IS THIS SCENE IMPORTANT?

A Shakespeare shows the themes of **loyalty** and **treachery** being discussed and demonstrated.

B We see the increasing **degradation** and **brutality** of Macbeth's reign: Banquo was assassinated for a purpose; Lady Macduff and her son, who are entirely innocent, are brutally murdered for **pure spite**.

C Shakespeare uses the scene with all its savagery to evoke our **pity** and **sympathy** for the victims.

D The character of **Ross** is that of the diplomat – always in the right place at the right time, and not a moment longer.

KEY CONNECTIONS

In Polanski's film version of *Macbeth* Ross, after leaving Lady Macduff, actively assists in the murder by opening the door to let the murderers in.

ACTION AND PROPHECY

It is not coincidental that the desire to eliminate all unfortunates that 'trace him in his line' (IV.1.153) immediately follows Macbeth's vision of the line of Banquo as kings – clearly, the thought of dynasty obsesses and torments Macbeth. At the same time, Shakespeare creates a scene which is affecting because the dialogue between Lady Macduff and her son reveals two delightful human beings: the waste of life that Macbeth's ambition has incurred is more fully realised in this snapshot of two good people about to be 'snuffed' out, than in all the talk about the stifling and tyrannical political atmosphere of Scotland under his reign.

But there is an even-handed justice which follows Macbeth's attempt to root out Macduff's 'line': just as Lady Macduff goes off stage screaming to her death, so subsequently Lady Macbeth screams off stage as she takes her own life. In Lady Macbeth's case, of course, Macbeth hears it. The train of events he has started effectively return to his own family, as Shakespeare makes clear.

EXAMINER'S TIP: WRITING ABOUT SHAKESPEARE'S DRAMATIC TECHNIQUES

We do not see Lady Macduff murdered on stage (unlike her son), but we do see and further hear her screaming *'Murder!'* as she flees off stage. This seems a particularly brilliant piece of staging by Shakespeare that reinforces a central thematic idea. To have had her murdered on stage would have created a moment of fear and suspense, but the execution would have been over immediately, and there would be another dead body left on the stage.

Structurally, to have her fleeing off stage, screaming murder, prolongs that sense of suspense – we are not certain she is dead until the next scene. This is a natural consequence of the kind of fear that Macbeth himself detests – not knowing, not being sure. His reign has created this unease for everybody.

Act IV Scene 3: Malcolm and Macduff discuss kingship

SUMMARY

- In England, Malcolm is suspicious of Macduff and pretends that he is even more evil than Macbeth.

- Macduff's lament for Scotland, however, convinces Malcolm – who then retracts his confessions of evil – that Macduff is sincere and opposed to Macbeth. He reveals to Macduff that he has English support for an invasion of Scotland.

- Macduff is confused but pleased by this turn of events. A doctor appears and mentions the saintly work of King Edward the Confessor.

- Ross arrives and informs Macduff that his family has been murdered.

- Macduff resolves to support Malcolm and vows to kill Macbeth himself.

WHY IS THIS SCENE IMPORTANT?

A We see – initially – the **fear** and **suspicion** created by Macbeth's reign in Scotland extended to England.

B Shakespeare provides a number of **important ideas** of what it means to be a **king**.

C Though static – a **'talking' scene** – Shakespeare skilfully creates considerable dramatic tension by depicting Malcolm playing his game with Macduff, and showing Ross reluctant to reveal the truth to Macduff.

D Shakespeare sets up and helps us **anticipate** the **final conflict** between Macbeth and Macduff.

E It provides a **balance** to the pure evil of scenes 1 and 2 in Act IV: visiting the witches, and the dreadful murder of the Macduffs. More **'normal' emotions** and reactions are depicted.

THE CHARACTERS OF MALCOLM, MACDUFF AND ROSS

Malcolm is suspicious of Macduff because, as he says, 'He hath not touched you yet' (line 14), meaning that Macbeth has not injured Macduff's family (a dramatic irony in the circumstances of the preceding scene), and so why should Macduff quarrel with Macbeth? Malcolm has already experienced traitors who have tried to entrap him (lines 117–20), and so is wary of committing himself.

Contrasting how characters react to similar events shows what they are like: Macduff's reaction to the death of his wife might usefully be compared with Macbeth's reaction (V.5.17–28). Shakespeare shows us how desensitised Macbeth has become to all normal human feeling. Finally, in trying to understand human character, we might want to ask why Ross, in relating the death of Macduff's family, does not mention his own presence and conversation with Lady Macduff and his 'cousin' (IV.2.25) shortly before.

EXAMINER'S TIP: WRITING ABOUT THE THEME OF KINGSHIP

One simple way of thinking about good versus evil kingship is the idea that good kings like Edward and Duncan, as Shakespeare makes clear, bestow blessings on their people, whereas everything Macbeth does gives a curse.

KEY QUOTE

'Such sanctity hath heaven given his hand, They presently amend.'

CHECKPOINT 12

Why does Malcolm pretend he is more evil than Macbeth?

★ **GRADE BOOSTER**

If you are asked about the nature of kingship (a key theme in the play) be sure to draw out and contrast the good and bad personal qualities from the full range of potential candidates, not just Macbeth and Duncan, but also Banquo, Edward and Malcolm. Adding a personal response on what you think the qualities of a good king are will be even more impressive.

KEY QUOTE

'All the perfumes of Arabia will not sweeten this little hand.'

Act V Scene 1: Lady Macbeth reveals her guilt while asleep

SUMMARY

1. In Macbeth's castle at Dunsinane a doctor and a waiting-gentlewoman discuss their patient, Lady Macbeth.

2. The gentlewoman refuses to discuss what she has heard Lady Macbeth say in her sleep, since she has no witness to back up her statements.

3. As the doctor attempts to persuade her, Lady Macbeth appears, sleep walking.

4. They both hear her reveal her guilt and watch her futile attempts to remove the blood from her hands.

5. The doctor concludes that she is in need of spiritual rather than medical attention.

WHY IS THIS SCENE IMPORTANT?

A It begins the **physical decline** of the Macbeth family, as Lady Macbeth is shown to be no longer in control.

B Shakespeare reveals how **ordinary people react** as they discover the enormity of the crimes committed by the Macbeths.

C Shakespeare brilliantly depicts the **psychological 'truth'** of a mental breakdown: the mental torture, the guilt and the obsession with the past.

D Shakespeare portrays Lady Macbeth's condition as very sad, but also clearly the result of her **own choices**.

E The **contrast** with Macbeth himself in Act V could not be more marked: 'I cannot taint with fear' (V.3.3), he says. Until the prophecies start unravelling, Macbeth seems completely resistant to worry of any sort.

GRADE BOOSTER

Original and creative thinking about character is very relevant here for achieving higher grades: consider the involvement or feelings of Lady Macbeth in the murder of Lady Macduff. Shakespeare does not explicitly link her to the decision to murder Lady Macduff, but she is clearly upset by the deed. Why do you think this is?

THE LANGUAGE OF BREAKDOWN

It is worth noting that Shakespeare wrote most of the play in blank verse. Notable exceptions are in the Porter's scene (Act II Scene 3) and this appearance of Lady Macbeth. Particularly in the first two Acts, Lady Macbeth's speech had been fiery blank verse – the strong rhythms reflecting her strong, determined grasp of reality. Now, she speaks in prose – choppy, abrupt, lurching from one incident to another, and even descending to doggerel with the rhyme of 'Fife' and 'wife' (line 38).

Shakespeare's writing here is brilliantly recreating what it means to 'break down'– the language is breaking down under the strain Lady Macbeth is under. It is therefore not surprising that she commits suicide – she can no longer hold 'it' together, and on death, of course, language disappears altogether. Note the contrast between the English court where the king heals 'Evil', and here where the disease is beyond the help of any doctor.

DRAMATIC IRONY

Shakespeare has Lady Macbeth say, 'What's done is done' (III.2.12), thus suggesting that it would no longer be of concern. Here, despite all her courage, ambition and strength of purpose, all that has been 'done' is not past, but present – and ever present – in her mind. She herself refers to her earlier words when she says, 'What's done cannot be undone' (lines 60–1).

Shakespeare, then, uses the device of deep dramatic irony to reveal her guilt: the physical symptoms of washing her hands reminding us of her earlier statement that 'A little water clears us of this deed' (II.2.65) and also of Macbeth's insight upon actually committing the murder that 'Will all great Neptune's ocean wash this blood / Clean from my hand? No' (II.2.57–8). Although they share a common aim (to gain the throne), their beliefs are different: ultimately, however, Shakespeare shows that all their beliefs are proved hollow.

? DID YOU KNOW

After the Restoration of Charles II, the language of Shakespeare went out of fashion. Shakespeare's godson, William Davenant, produced versions of the plays which became more popular than Shakespeare's own (from 1674 to 1744).

Act V Scene 2: Macbeth's enemies prepare to fight

SUMMARY

❶ Knowing that Malcolm is marching north with a troop of English soldiers, we are introduced to the rebel Scottish powers who are determined to overthrow Macbeth.

❷ They plan to meet up with the English at Birnam Wood.

❸ The thanes comment on how uneasy Macbeth must now feel, as his inadequacies and guilt must face the test – and they are confident of victory.

KEY QUOTE

'Now does he feel his title Hang loose about him, like a giant's robe Upon a dwarfish thief.'

WHY IS THIS SCENE IMPORTANT?

A Shakespeare moves us from the **prospect** of action at the close of Act IV to the **actual** hurly-burly of war – plans, preparations and advances.

B Shakespeare uses this scene to help **accelerate** the build-up – we are anxious for the **climax**.

C We learn how **desperate** Macbeth's situation is: nobody supports him.

D Shakespeare's mention of Birnam Wood and Dunsinane **reminds** us of the **prophecies**.

E Not only the English, but also the Scots are involved in **cleansing** Scotland.

PLAYING TO THE CROWN

Shakespeare ensures that the recovery of the crown by Malcolm is not solely through English forces; this is important, particularly bearing in mind that James (the First of England and Sixth of Scotland) was an audience for the play. Scotland, too, played an important role in casting off its tyrannical yoke. In today's terms, Shakespeare was being 'politically correct' in drawing attention to the fact.

EXAMINER'S TIP: WRITING ABOUT THE IMAGERY OF CLOTHING

Notice how Shakespeare deliberately uses the imagery of clothing once more (lines 20–2) – Macbeth is simply not big enough to hold onto the crown.

Act V Scene 3: Macbeth is not afraid

SUMMARY

1. Macbeth enters with the doctor and attendants.

2. He is in a fearless mood: the prophecies give him complete confidence that he is untouchable.

3. A servant is jeered as he reports that the English troops are arriving.

4. Macbeth orders his armour and asks the doctor to cure his wife.

5. He curtly dismisses the doctor's medical advice and asks him instead what would cure his country.

6. He scarcely listens to the doctor's reply – he is obsessed with the prophecies, which he thinks are the only things that will guarantee his security.

WHY IS THIS SCENE IMPORTANT?

A Shakespeare shows Macbeth as **fearless**, but also **desperate** – he has come to totally depend on the **prophecies** as his sole source of information and support.

B To understand that Macbeth has begun a **reign of terror** is one thing, but in this scene we see how Shakespeare shows that terror in very particular terms: Macbeth's treatment of and **contempt** for ordinary people and servants – those around him – all contribute to the sense of his increasing **lack of support**.

C Shakespeare, by placing a doctor first with Lady Macbeth, now with Macbeth himself, demonstrates the wider theme that the country needs healing under Macbeth's kingship.

MACBETH'S TRAGEDY

Shakespeare re-introduces the doctor from Act V Scene 1, providing a neat sense of continuity and dramatic irony: the question of ministering to Lady Macbeth extends to the wider issue of ministering to the country, which has, as Macbeth notes, a 'disease' (line 51). Yet despite that, there is a part of him which still evokes compassion: his recognition of the life he might have had – which included 'honour', 'love' and 'troops of friends' (lines 24–5) – cannot but touch the heart. He knows, and relishes, what is good – but has chosen the opposite. This is his tragedy.

That Macbeth is doomed should be obvious from this scene alone: the dependence he now has on the prophecies is paralysing his own decision-making and capacity for action. 'Bring me no more reports' (line 1) is a desperate statement for someone engaged in a war to utter – intelligence-gathering is of primary importance. Shakespeare has him begin and end the scene reciting the prophecies – they have become a mantra to him. On them and them alone his survival depends.

EXAMINER'S TIP: WRITING ABOUT MACBETH'S DISEASE

Remember that the political aspect of treachery is never very far away, as Shakespeare demonstrates. The comments on Lady Macbeth's health, mostly made by Macbeth to the doctor, apply equally to Macbeth himself. But he, of course, will have 'none of it' (line 47). Instead his restless energy seeks violent outlets – the casual way he orders the hanging of anyone talking of fear (line 36) shows how callous and depraved he has become.

KEY QUOTE

'Till Birnam wood remove to Dunsinane I cannot taint with fear.'

? DID YOU KNOW

William Davenant's version of 'The devil damn thee black, thou cream-faced loon: / Where got'st thou that goose look?' (V.3.11–12) was: 'Now Friend, what means thy change of countenance?' Which do you prefer?

Act V Scene 4: Birnam Wood moves

SUMMARY

❶ Malcolm orders his men to each cut down a bough from Birnam Wood and to carry it in front of them as they march in order to conceal their numbers from Macbeth.

❷ They learn that Macbeth intends to remain in Dunsinane, his strategy being to endure a siege.

❸ This is his only hope, since his troops are demoralised and fight for him out of necessity, not commitment.

KEY QUOTE

'And none serve with him but constrainèd things Whose hearts are absent too.'

WHY IS THIS SCENE IMPORTANT?

A Shakespeare creates **tension** by showing us the preparations going on in the camp opposing Macbeth.

B We are reminded of the **prophecy** in the reference to the Wood.

C The witches only appear in four scenes (and two of these extremely briefly), but their influence – and that of the **supernatural** – is felt throughout the play.

Examiner's tip: Writing about Shakespeare's stagecraft

Notice how Shakespeare creates a neat structure, which simply and effectively increases tension. Scene 1 led us into the diseased mind of Lady Macbeth; in Scene 2 we switched to the preparation of the Scottish thanes who were planning to attack Macbeth. Scene 3 returned us to the castle. This time we witnessed Macbeth's diseased mind, but were also made much more aware of Scotland's disease.

Now, in Scene 4, we return to the cure for all these diseases: the English army led by Malcolm, the rightful king. As Siward concludes: 'certain issue strokes must arbitrate' (line 20) – a bloody operation to remove the disease by lopping it off. We have seen, therefore, the situation in both camps – and we note the contrasts. Now the battle must commence. Writing about how a playwright like Shakespeare carefully structures the play to create added impact and increase tension can get you high marks.

KEY CONNECTIONS

Tales from Shakespeare by Marion Williams (1998) includes *Macbeth*. This is a modern retelling with excellent illustrations and some quotations from the play.

Act V Scene 5: Lady Macbeth dies

SUMMARY

KEY QUOTE

'Life's but a walking shadow, a poor player That struts and frets his hour upon the stage, And then is heard no more.'

① Macbeth enters boasting that his castle can easily endure a siege: he is confident of victory.

② Macbeth's confidence in his strategy – bolstered by the witches' prophecy – is in marked contrast to the humility present in Malcolm's camp.

③ Macbeth regrets that he cannot go out to face the traitors – too many of his men have gone over to the other side.

④ A woman's scream is heard and Seyton goes to investigate. Macbeth reflects that nothing terrifies him now.

⑤ Seyton returns and informs Macbeth that his wife has died. For him this is a confirmation that life is meaningless.

⑥ A messenger arrives to tell him that Birnam Wood is moving towards Dunsinane Castle.

⑦ Outraged, and in some considerable doubt about his destiny and the meaning of the prophecies, he immediately changes his strategy and orders an attack.

WHY IS THIS SCENE IMPORTANT?

A The queen commits suicide – the final end of her **ambitions** – and Shakespeare shows us Macbeth reflecting on the meaninglessness of it all.

B The prophecies start **unravelling**, and Macbeth, who has so blindly followed them, is derailed from his key strategy to hold the castle. Thus, ironically, Shakespeare shows us that accepting the prophecy leads directly to Macbeth's downfall.

C **Courage** – going out to face his enemies and fight them – becomes again Macbeth's key characteristic.

CHECKPOINT 13

How do the prophecies destroy Macbeth?

EXAMINER'S TIP: WRITING ABOUT LADY MACBETH'S DEATH

Shakespeare portrays Lady Macbeth's death as inevitable from all the comments made in Act V. But there was no point in showing it on stage – it is much more effective (and neatly symmetrical when we consider Lady Macduff's end) to hear her final scream. The interest of her death is in Macbeth's reaction to it. This can be read in a number of ways:

● Is he entirely indifferent and emotionless – 'Signifying nothing' (line 28)?

● Does his **soliloquy** suggest mere cynicism as a last response – 'Told by an idiot' (line 27)?

● Or does the word 'hereafter' (line 17) signify his realisation of the real loss in his life?

Whichever might be true, and Shakespeare presents it so that they are not exclusive, there is something in the isolation that he is suffering that cannot help but move us to pity him, despite our revulsion for all that he stands for. Notice Macbeth's state of mind: 'I 'gin to be aweary of the sun' (line 49) – he no longer cares whether he lives or dies.

GRADE BOOSTER

Focus on specific ideas in your essay which you then expand to make a broader point. For example, contrast the deaths of Lady Macduff and Lady Macbeth, and explore the reactions of their husbands, to make clear you understand the differences in their characters.

Act V Scenes 6–9: The death of Macbeth

SUMMARY

❶ (Scene 6): Malcolm, Macduff and Siward, with their armies camouflaged, approach Macbeth's castle. Battle commences.

❷ (Scene 7): Macbeth kills Young Siward in combat. He is trapped but unbeaten, even though his army has fallen.

❸ (Scene 8): Macbeth encounters Macduff, who reveals that he was not 'born' of woman (line 13), but delivered by Caesarian (lines 15–16). In a final act of courage Macbeth fights Macduff and is killed.

❹ (Scene 9): While Malcolm comforts Siward over the death of his son, Macduff arrives with Macbeth's head and hails Malcolm King of Scotland.

WHY ARE THESE SCENES IMPORTANT?

A Shakespeare shows the full extent of Macbeth's duping by the witches.
B Our curiosity about the prophecies – especially of someone not born of a woman – is satisfied.
C Despite all the witches have done to enslave Macbeth, Shakespeare demonstrates that his courage still remains.
D The waste and pointlessness of Macbeth's reign is summarised in the death of Young Siward.

MACBETH AS WARRIOR

Shakespeare presents Macbeth primarily as a warrior, and this is important in our final evaluation of him: through giving in to the temptation that the witches offered him, they succeeded in destroying almost every aspect of his true humanity. Even his courage temporarily deserts him (V.8.18) when he learns from Macduff how false the prophecies are – yet his courage returns: he will not yield. He will take on Fate as well as Macduff – 'Yet I will try the last' (V.8.32) – and this, while it does not excuse his crimes, does enable us to see some remnant of his great bravery.

Shakespeare establishes early on Macbeth's ferocious qualifications as a fighter – if we have forgotten about this, because subsequently Macbeth operates through murderers, then in this final scene we are reminded of where his true strength is. This is important – otherwise Macduff's achievement in slaying him in one-to-one combat is diminished.

MACBETH AND THE WITCHES

Macbeth's analysis of the prophesies of the witches – 'these juggling fiends' (V.8.19) comes full circle: he was warned by Banquo (I.3.121–5) and now he has experienced and knows exactly what Banquo predicted. Further, juggling in a 'double sense' (V.8.20) refers to words having two meanings, which runs through the play.

Ironically, just as Macbeth betrayed Duncan, so the witches have betrayed Macbeth. When deliberating the pros and cons of treason and murder Macbeth commented 'we but teach / Bloody instructions, which, being taught, return / To plague th' inventor' (I.7.8–10). Shakespeare shows this, too, has come true – he has had no rest as his own men and thanes have constantly defected from his cause, and his ultimate trust in the witches also proves misplaced.

? DID YOU KNOW

The themes of revenge and retribution feature strongly in Greek Tragedy.

KEY QUOTE

'And be these juggling fiends no more believed That palter with us in a double sense – That keep the word of promise to our ear, And break it to our hope!' [V.8.19–22]

Progress and revision check

REVISION ACTIVITY

1 Who is informed by the witches that his sons will be kings? (Write your answers below)

....

2 Why is Macbeth upset when Duncan announces the identity of the 'Prince of Cumberland'?

....

3 What happens when Lady Macbeth receives a letter from her husband?

....

4 Who abandons his wife and children and flees to England?

....

5 How does Macbeth change his plans when Birnam Wood comes to Dunsinane?

....

REVISION ACTIVITY

On a piece of paper write down answers to these questions:

● How do Macbeth's actions in the first half of the play return to haunt him in the second half?

Start: *We know that Macbeth, in considering murdering Duncan, understands the possible consequences ...*

● How important is Lady Macbeth's role in Macbeth's rise to power?

Start: *Lady Macbeth's role is initially critical in persuading Macbeth to suppress his conscience ...*

GRADE BOOSTER ★

Answer this longer, practice question about the plot/action of the play.

Q: In what ways do the witches contribute to the action of the play?

Think about ...

● The way that events or actions are repeated or mirrored

● The way that events slowly build up to a climax

For a C grade: convey your ideas clearly and appropriately (you could use words from the question to guide your answer) and refer to details from the text (use specific examples).

For an A grade: comment on the varied contributions the witches make, and consider original or alternative interpretations, such as whether, had the witches not existed, Macbeth would have committed evil acts regardless.

PART THREE: CHARACTERS

Macbeth

WHO IS MACBETH?

Macbeth is a warrior and the Thane of Glamis, whose ambitions lead him to betray and murder his king, and take the throne of Scotland.

WHAT DOES MACBETH DO IN THE PLAY?

- Macbeth defeats the armies of the rebellion against King Duncan (I.2).

- After meeting three witches, Macbeth plots with his wife, Lady Macbeth, to murder Duncan and assume the throne (I.7, II.2, 4).

- Macbeth has his friend, Banquo, murdered (III.2, 3) in order to prevent Banquo's children becoming kings, as predicted by the witches. After receiving fresh prophecies from the witches, he destroys Macduff's family.

- Cornered by English and Scottish forces, realising the prophecies have betrayed him, Macbeth is killed in single combat by Macduff.

HOW IS MACBETH DESCRIBED AND WHAT DOES IT MEAN?

Quotation	Means?
'For brave Macbeth – well he deserves that name'	Macbeth is first and foremost a warrior – courage is his defining quality.
'yet do I fear thy nature; / It is too full o' the milk of human kindness / To catch the nearest way'	Suggests someone who is too kind, too soft, to achieve the top positions in life.
'Thou hast it now: king, Cawdor, Glamis, all, / As the weird women promised, and, I fear, / Thou play'dst most foully for't'	While others have been blamed for murdering King Duncan, the circumstances indicate that Macbeth is deceitful and responsible for the murder.
'this dead butcher'	Finally, Macbeth becomes nothing but a mass murderer.

EXAMINER'S TIP: WRITING ABOUT MACBETH

When you are writing about Macbeth always remember that the play is the 'tragedy' of Macbeth. In other words, Shakespeare does not present him as a wholly bad person – he began the play with admirable qualities but, under the influence of the witches and his wife, he changed. Thus you need to balance his final condition – the treacherous, mass murderer under the sway of supernatural forces – with his earlier and finer qualities: his love of his wife, his sensitive imagination and bravery. Ask, what remains at the end? Ensure your answer is balanced.

★ GRADE BOOSTER

To boost your own ideas, find two more quotations about Macbeth. Draw your own table and write in the second column what you think each quotation means.

🔒 EXAMINER'S TIP

The witches are evil; God is good; Macbeth is human, and so a mixture of good and evil. This is what interests us about him. In writing about Macbeth focus on how he is tempted. Contrast him with how Banquo is tempted, but does not give way.

⭐ **GRADE BOOSTER**

Come up with your own interpretations for key quotations. What motivation might Malcolm have in simply calling Lady Macbeth a 'fiend-like queen' rather than referring to her feelings of guilt, or acknowledging that she didn't, herself, kill anyone directly?

Lady Macbeth

WHO IS LADY MACBETH?

Lady Macbeth is the ambitious wife of Macbeth, who encourages him to murder his king, helps him to do it, and so becomes queen of Scotland.

WHAT DOES SHE DO IN THE PLAY?

- She invokes the powers of evil to help her influence her husband (I.5, I.7) to commit murder and treason.

- Subsequently, she acts the perfect hostess to the king in a false display of duty and affection (I.6).

- She is an accomplice in the murder and in establishing the 'guilt' of Duncan's guards (II.2); she is also crucial in the 'cover-up' (II.3). Her quick thinking and presence of mind also saves Macbeth from admitting his guilt to the thanes when Banquo's ghost appears at their banquet (III.4).

- Increasingly isolated from her husband, Lady Macbeth sleep walks (V.1), obsessed with nightmares of her actions, and finally commits suicide (V.5).

HOW IS SHE DESCRIBED AND WHAT DOES IT MEAN?

Quotation	Means?
'Fair and noble hostess' and 'most kind hostess'	Duncan describes Lady Macbeth as the gracious wife of one of his most important lords.
'my dearest partner of greatness' and 'my dearest chuck'	Macbeth initially has affection for his wife, and trusts her to help him with his plans.
'Bring forth men-children only; For thy undaunted mettle should compose Nothing but males'	Macbeth compliments his wife by saying her strength makes her like a man. There is nothing 'soft' or feminine in her.
'fiend-like queen'	Malcolm's final judgement is that Lady Macbeth was like a fiend – a devil in fact.

🔓 **EXAMINER'S TIP**

Lady Macbeth is dominant, cunning, determined and haunted. These four aspects could make up the core elements of an essay response on her character.

EXAMINER'S TIP: WRITING ABOUT LADY MACBETH 🔓

Remember: Shakespeare does not present Lady Macbeth as equal to Macbeth – it is not *their* tragedy, but his. Her role, however, is vital and also supplementary to the work of the witches: Macbeth is tempted to do evil and Lady Macbeth is the key human agent – the one Macbeth trusts and loves – who ensures his temptation is thorough and complete. Despite her initial overpowering presence, she is not a heroine herself. This is shown when she collapses once Macbeth withdraws his confidence from her.

Banquo

WHO IS BANQUO?

Banquo is the honourable and loyal friend and thane who is tempted like Macbeth, but who resists the temptation only to be subsequently murdered by Macbeth.

WHAT DOES BANQUO DO IN THE PLAY?

- Banquo helps defeat the enemies of King Duncan in battle (I.2).
- The witches give prophecies to him as well as Macbeth (I.3).
- He warns Macbeth of the possible consequences of trusting the prophecies (I.3).
- He suspects something before and after the murder (II.1, II.3, III.1).
- Banquo is assassinated at Macbeth's orders while out riding with his son (III.3).
- He appears as a ghost to Macbeth and disrupts his celebrations (III.4).
- Finally, he appears as an apparition to Macbeth confirming that his offspring will become future kings of Scotland and more (IV.1).

HOW IS BANQUO DESCRIBED AND WHAT DOES IT MEAN?

Quotation	Means?
'Lesser than Macbeth, and greater'	He will not become king himself, but his descendants will.
'Noble Banquo, That hast no less deserved, nor must be known No less to have done so'	The king appreciates Banquo's qualities and honours him – the word 'noble' suggests generosity of spirit, warmth and compassion.
'If you shall cleave to my consent, when 'tis, It shall make honour for you'	Macbeth is tempting Banquo's loyalty to the king, and Banquo in his reply makes it clear that he is loyal and commited to the king.
'in his royalty of nature Reigns that which would be fear'd . . . He hath a wisdom that doth guide his valour'	Banquo is genuinely a superior person – with qualities of boldness, discretion and understanding that make him a dangerous adversary to Macbeth.

EXAMINER'S TIP: WRITING ABOUT BANQUO

If Macbeth succumbs to evil forces and suggestions, then Banquo is his opposite. Shakespeare presents both as warriors and thanes, both see and hear the witches, but Banquo resists acting on their prophecies; at every point he seems to stand up for honour and integrity. However, one weakness proves to be his undoing: knowing of the prophecies, suspecting that Macbeth has 'play'dst most foully for't', why doesn't he reveal what he knows? This omission costs him his life: he fails to realise he will be the next victim, given his knowledge.

GRADE BOOSTER

Look for original and powerful connections between characters. For example, Banquo and Macduff are linked by more than opposition to Macbeth: Banquo is the 'Caesar' (III.1) whose power intimidates Macbeth; Macduff is actually born from a Caesarean (V.8) operation – the key aspect of the prophecy that will undo Macbeth.

GLOSSARY

cleave has two opposite meanings – 1) to divide or split and 2) to unite or adhere

★ GRADE BOOSTER

It is easy to see characters in 'black and white' – Macduff as strong, loyal and forthright – but if you can show why Shakespeare creates an impact through subtle distinctions, then all the better. Macduff is distressed when he is told of his family's death (IV.3.204–30) – which could be seen, in a warrior, as a form of weakness.

Macduff

WHO IS MACDUFF?

Macduff is the honourable thane – the man of destiny, 'not born of woman' – who ultimately brings retribution to Macbeth.

WHAT DOES MACDUFF DO IN THE PLAY?

- He discovers Duncan's murder (II.3).

- Macduff suspects Macbeth's guilt and refuses to attend his coronation (II.4). Macbeth begins to fear him (III.iv).

- Macduff abandons his castle and flies to England without his family (IV.1). His family are murdered in his absence (IV.2).

- He hunts out and kills Macbeth in single combat (V.8).

HOW IS MACDUFF DESCRIBED AND WHAT DOES IT MEAN?

Quotation	Means?
'Dear Duff'	Macduff is held in esteem and affection by his peers.
'Then live, Macduff: what need I fear of thee?'	Macbeth goes from hot to cold in his reaction to Macduff; at his deepest level he knows he should fear Macduff – a warrior too – which is why he attempts to destroy him.
'His flight was madness: when our actions do not, Our fears do make us traitors.'	There is something impulsive in Macduff's behaviour, something irrational – why would you leave your wife and children?
'Macduff, this noble passion . . . thy good truth and honour.'	At root Macduff is a passionate and true man – someone who can be trusted.

🔒 EXAMINER'S TIP

Before the examination, spend at least five minutes focusing and relaxing. This helps put you in the right frame of mind.

EXAMINER'S TIP: WRITING ABOUT MACDUFF

Shakespeare, in Macduff's flight to England, shows us two aspects of his character: he illustrates his 'noble passion / Child of integrity' (IV.3.114–15) and also raises the question of his judgement. Lady Macduff thinks his flight is cowardice; Malcolm initially finds it so difficult to accept that he treats Macduff with extreme suspicion. Was it the right thing to do? Were the affairs of state more important than family considerations? Is Macduff calculating in some sort of political way? Balance his passion for justice with his flight to England – did he simply not foresee the extent of savagery that Macbeth would exercise on his family?

The witches

WHO ARE THE WITCHES?

The witches embody demonic intelligences which are scarcely human; they provide information, but do not directly invite human beings to commit crimes.

WHAT DO THE WITCHES DO IN THE PLAY?

The witches seem evil and appear to provide information about the future (I.3, IV.1) which destabilises the present by tempting Macbeth.

HOW ARE THE WITCHES DESCRIBED AND WHAT DOES IT MEAN?

Quotation	Means?
'And oftentimes to win us to our harm, The instruments of darkness tell us truths'	The agents of evil are deceptive and dangerous, and even use truth itself to produce a terrible outcome.
'Infected be the air whereon they ride, And damn'd all those that trust them'	The witches, as Macbeth observes, are infected or diseased and those who trust them will catch the illness – as Macbeth does.
'Would they had stay'd'	There is something about their message which is compelling and attractive.
'Call 'em, let me see 'em'	The witches themselves are controlled by higher supernatural powers

EXAMINER'S TIP: WRITING ABOUT THE WITCHES

In writing about the witches focus on how Shakespeare presents them: are they human at all, are they male or female, and can they be said to have human characters? Shakespeare has them embody evil and demonic intelligence. This, of necessity, is fixed and elemental: they do not change, unlike Macbeth.

Their information tempts Macbeth – but notice that they do not invite him to murder Duncan or even suggest that he does. Information is morally neutral until human beings begin to interpret it. Thus they symbolise evil, but man is free to resist them. Macbeth is tragic partly because he comes to depend upon their information.

Malcolm, Lady Macduff and Ross

WHO ARE THEY?

● **Malcolm** is the son of Duncan, heir to the throne, falsely framed by Macbeth for murdering Duncan; he returns with an English army to reclaim the throne.

● **Lady Macduff** is the brave wife of Macduff, who does not run away, despite warnings; she is murdered with her son by criminals sent by Macbeth.

● **Ross** is an enigmatic thane who always seems to be on the right side of self-preservation.

WHAT DO THEY DO IN THE PLAY?

● Malcolm outlines true kingly virtues (IV.3) to Macduff and replaces Macbeth as king.

● Lady Macduff shows the qualities of a loving mother and wife (IV.2).

● Ross brings news (I.3, IV.3), but his motives are always questionable.

HOW ARE THEY DESCRIBED AND WHAT DOES IT MEAN?

GRADE BOOSTER

Don't forget the importance of King Duncan in the play – even though he disappears after the end of Act I. For discussion of Duncan see **Part Two: Act I Scene 6.**

Quotation	Means?
'Hail king, for so thou art'	**Malcolm**, the real king, at last has the crown.
'My dearest coz'	**Lady Macduff** is loved by her family and friends.
'Well may you see things well done there: adieu.'	**Ross** is to attend Macbeth's coronation – he will fit in with the new order, and not 'rock the boat'.

EXAMINER'S TIP: WRITING ABOUT MINOR CHARACTERS

Contrasting the minor characters with the major ones often throws extra light on them: Malcolm's innocence with Macbeth's corruption, Lady Macduff's murder off stage with Lady Macbeth's suicide off stage, Ross's compliance with Macduff's stubborness. The Porter, who appears in Act II Scene 3, is a marvellously comic character, with his own special purpose. The marvel is in how Shakespeare bends even the Porter's language to serve the themes of the play – while simultaneously giving Macbeth an opportunity to wash and change clothing before re-appearing on stage.

Progress and revision check

REVISION ACTIVITY

1. What 'spurs' Macbeth on to murder Duncan? (Write your answers below)

....

2. Whose character is most like the serpent concealed by the innocent flower?

....

3. Who strongly resists 'cursed thoughts'?

....

4. Which character is mostly concerned with justice and fairness?

....

5. Whose kingship demonstrates he has been 'clear in his great office'?

....

REVISION ACTIVITY

On a piece of paper write down answers to these questions:

● How does Shakespeare convey Macbeth's character change during the course of the play?

Start: *Initially, Shakespeare presents Macbeth as a hero-warrior, loyal to his king and cause, who is fully aware of the horrors and implications of treason ...*

● What is Lady Macbeth's influence on her husband's character?

Start: *Lady Macbeth plays a major role in influencing Macbeth and exploiting his 'deep desires' so that the worst side of his nature is revealed ...*

GRADE BOOSTER ★

Answer this longer, practice question about the characters of the play.

Q: Macbeth and Banquo start the play as two fighting heroes, but their destinies are very different – compare their characters and show how their differences lead to such different results.

Think about ...

● The way they each respond to events they both experience

● The way they describe their experiences

For a C grade: convey your comparisons clearly and appropriately and refer to details from the text (use specific examples).

For an A grade: make sure you comment on the varied ways the characters are revealed, and ensure that the two characters are directly and frequently contrasted. Explore original or alternative interpretations, for example considering whether Banquo is as noble as he is often presented.

PART FOUR: KEY CONTEXTS AND THEMES

Key contexts

? DID YOU KNOW

A complete collection of Shakespeare's plays was only published seven years after his death, in 1623.

SHAKESPEARE'S LIFE

Born in Stratford-upon-Avon in 1564, William Shakespeare died there almost exactly fifty-two years later, in 1616. During those fifty-two years he created at least thirty-seven plays and possibly had a hand in others. He was also to write several poems, including his famous Sonnets.

King James I of England

Macbeth was written some time between 1603 and 1606. This coincides with the accession of James the Sixth of Scotland to the English throne, as James the First of England, in 1603. The play was certainly written with James primarily in mind and there is a story that the king 'was pleas'd with his own Hand to write an amicable letter to Mr Shakespeare'.

The play is written with James's interests in mind: it echoes his fascination with the supernatural (witches and prophecies); it compliments him by making his ancestor, Banquo, a hero in the play (IV.1). Further, as he had survived an assassination attempt, questions about the monarchs' role and the duties of their subjects towards them were ever in the forefront of his mind (as Macbeth is aware: I.7). Finally, the play is intimately related to the topical events of the Gunpowder Plot of 1605 and the subsequent trials of its conspirators (II.3).

Succession and order

Of great importance in Shakespeare's time was the political issue of succession (deciding who would be the next king or queen). Elizabeth remained the 'Virgin' Queen throughout her reign, which meant she had no natural successor. This created more instability: for example the Essex rising of 1601 was a symptom of the need for political certainty (Shakespeare's friend and patron the Earl of Southampton was involved in the uprising and was imprisoned as a result). Elizabeth herself did not name her successor till she actually came to her death-bed.

Thus, rebellion and anarchy had to be avoided in future – hence the importance of order, 'degree' (rank) and loyalty. We see a reference to it at Macbeth's feast. He invites his assembled guests to sit down: 'You know your own degrees' (III.4.1). Where one sat was determined by rank. By divine appointment, the king ruled over men and to violate or seek to violate this situation was against God's Will, thereby producing 'unnatural' results. Thus, the unnatural killing of Duncan is accompanied by, among other things, 'A falcon [a royal bird] towering in her pride of place' which is 'by a mousing owl [an inferior bird] hawked at, and killed' (II.4.12–13).

SETTING AND PLACE

The play is set mostly in Scotland – the exception being IV.3 where Macduff joins Malcolm in England. The action takes place either outdoors – the witches on the heath, the murder of Banquo, the English army advancing – or within castle walls – the planning to murder Duncan, the murder of Duncan, the murder of Lady Macduff, the sleep walking of Lady Macbeth and so on. This gives the play two contrasting qualities: outdoors there is an elemental sense of force and nature; within the castle there is a sense of claustrophobic evil, as more is planned or as supernatural events – Banquo's ghost – interrupt a banquet.

EXAMINER'S TIP: WRITING ABOUT SETTING AND PLACE

Shakespeare has written a play – a fiction – but one of the reasons that it seems so realistic and compelling is his use of setting and place. The castles – perhaps true to their military origins – become places of bloodshed and suffering: Glamis is where Duncan is murdered; Dunsinane is where Macbeth defends the realm and is killed; Fife is where Macduff's family is slaughtered. On the other hand, Scone is a holy place, and Colmekill (Island of Iona) is where Duncan is buried. Add to this the place names – Birnam Wood (and Dunsinane) – occurring in the prophecies, then we can sense a kind of life or death force that each place seems to possess.

Key themes

AMBITION

Ambition is the fundamental theme not only because it is the driving force of Macbeth's life, and so of all the other themes, but also because it is the theme (in this play) which informs the Shakespearean idea of tragedy. In *Macbeth* we find that the hero's greatest weakness (causing Macbeth to fall from grace and inevitably die) is ambition.

Macbeth acknowledges this specifically when he is attempting to resist the murder of Duncan. This acknowledgement comes after he has considered all the good reasons for not murdering Duncan – only ambition is left to overrule his troubled conscience. Furthermore, while the influence of both Lady Macbeth and the witches is strong, their power over Macbeth is only possible because the ambition is already there.

On first meeting Macbeth we find him being startled and seeming to fear something which sounds 'so fair' (I.3.53) and this can only be because his ambition has caused him already to entertain treasonous thoughts. Macbeth, then, is a hero but one who is fatally undermined by his ambition, and the consequences of such ambition are the fabric of the play.

REVISION ACTIVITY

Below are examples where the theme of ambition occurs in the play. Can you think of any others?

- 'The Prince of Cumberland! That is a step
  On which I must fall down, or else o'erleap,
  For in my way it lies.' **(I.4.48–50)**

- 'I have no spur ... but only
  Vaulting ambition which o'erleaps itself' **(I.7.25–7)**

- 'For mine own good
  All causes shall give way' **(III.4.135–6)**

DID YOU KNOW

In Shakespeare's time authority derived from God – in a 'great chain of being'. God was at the top. Then angels, mankind, animals, birds, fish and so on. In the human order the king was supreme. Males were above females. Thus, questioning the will of a king had religious as well as political significance.

? **DID YOU KNOW**

The fall of the Earl of Essex during the reign of Elizabeth I happened only five years prior to *Macbeth* being written. Essex was perceived as being ambitious.

EXAMINER'S TIP: WRITING ABOUT AMBITION

Remember that ambition is the key theme of the play – Macbeth's 'tragedy' is caused by his ambition. But also ambition is explored through his wife, who is similarly inclined. We can contrast their approaches to ambition: she is strong initially while Macbeth wavers, and finally he is strong while she breaks down.

THE SUPERNATURAL

The supernatural (and witchcraft in particular), raises all sorts of questions concerning appearances and reality. Does the supernatural really exist and have such powers? Or, more precisely, did Shakespeare believe in them?

In Shakespeare's time witchcraft was a major issue: James the First believed in witchcraft. People generally believed in it, and it was a capital offence to be a witch, because they were considered enemies to society. Thus, we could argue that within the play the witches are real, and any attempt to present the play purely in psychological terms does not match Shakespeare's conception.

So, when Lady Macbeth calls on the dark forces (I.5) she is quite literally asking demonic spirits to possess her mind and body so that all human pity can be removed. It is important to convey, as Shakespeare intended, the sense of supernatural forces in the play.

REVISION ACTIVITY

Below are examples where the theme of the supernatural occurs in the play. Can you think of any others?

- 'Is this a dagger which I see before me' (II.1.33)
- 'Prithee, see there! Behold! Look! Lo – how say you?' [Banquo's ghost] (III.4.69)
- 'Out, damned spot! Out, I say!' (V.1.31)

EXAMINER'S TIP: WRITING ABOUT THE SUPERNATURAL

In writing about the supernatural the best marks will be for those who can explore how Shakespeare presents evil in such a way that it affects human beings, but is not in itself responsible for their actions. This is clearly shown by the parallel careers of Banquo and Macbeth – both are tempted, but Banquo resists the temptation to 'make' prophecy come true.

REVENGE

Revenge is an important theme and is contrasted with the idea of justice being done. When Duncan asks whether Cawdor has been executed (I.4.1), then, he is asking for justice to be done on a traitor. However, the execution of Duncan's guards by Macbeth is not justice, but – claims Macbeth deceptively – revenge for Duncan's murder. So begins a series of 'revenges'.

'Blood will have blood' (III.4.122) says Macbeth explicitly, aware that Banquo is seeking revenge even as a ghost for his murder. Later, as a ghost, Banquo 'smiles' (IV.1.123) at Macbeth, showing that his revenge is complete in the knowledge that his descendants will be kings.

Perhaps most importantly of all in terms of the play is Macduff's vengeance. By murdering Macduff's family Macbeth sets against himself the one man who can defeat him. Macduff's mission for revenge is entirely personal – he promises that Macbeth escaping from him is as likely as heaven forgiving him (IV.3.233–4).

REVISION ACTIVITY

Below are examples where the theme of revenge occurs in the play. Can you think of any others?

- 'There, the murderers,
  Steeped in the colours of their trade! – their daggers
  Unmannerly breeched with gore. Who could refrain' (II.3.110–12)

- 'It will have blood; they say, blood will have blood' (III.4.122)

- 'Front to front
  Bring thou this fiend of Scotland' (IV.3.231–2)

EXAMINER'S TIP: WRITING ABOUT REVENGE

Another way of considering the pattern of revenge in the play is by asking who in the family has been affected by Macbeth's actions. Consider that Malcolm (and Donalbain) have lost their father, as has Fleance, so the sons want revenge. Also, Macduff and Old Siward have lost their sons: they too will seek retribution. Macbeth hopes that murdering Duncan can be the 'be-all' and 'end-all' (I.7.5) of the matter – revenge is not so easily set aside.

WITCHCRAFT

Witchcraft is part of the supernatural theme of the play, and deserves separate mention, despite the fact that the witches themselves only appear in four scenes (I.1, I.3, III.5, IV.1). They are the first people we meet and their evil sets the scene for everything to come: thunder and lightning suggest the havoc that Scotland is about to experience. They know they will tell Macbeth something that will prey on his mind.

The knowledge that the witches supply is like a drug to Macbeth. He is fascinated by it at the start – 'would they had stayed' (I.3.83) – and continually wants more. This leads him to seek them out later in the play. Banquo warns him that you can't trust supernatural knowledge, but Macbeth will not listen.

Witchcraft has four functions in the play: it exposes the evil hiding in Macbeth; it directs his evil to particular deeds; it highlights the forces of evil at work in the world; and it creates a powerful atmosphere in the play.

DID YOU KNOW

King James hated witchcraft. In 1592 he interrogated the witch Agnes Sampson. He was astounded when she privately revealed to him the words he and his wife had spoken in bed together on the first night of their marriage. James 'swore by the living God that he believed all the devils in Hell could not have discovered the same'.

EXAMINER'S TIP

Small details of comparison can impress examiners: notice how Macbeth loves *supernatural* revelations, which Banquo rejects – Banquo is a lover of *nature* (I.4) instead.

REVISION ACTIVITY

Below are examples where the theme of witchcraft occurs in the play. Can you think of any others?

● 'Fair is foul, and foul is fair' (I.1.11)

● 'And oftentimes, to win us to our harm,
The instruments of darkness tell us truths' (I.3.124–5)

● 'Thither he
Will come to know his destiny' (III.5.16–17)

● 'Thou hast harped my fear aright. But one word more' (IV.1.74)

EXAMINER'S TIP: WRITING ABOUT WITCHCRAFT

One of the cleverest ways that Shakespeare shows the power and influence of witchcraft is by using language to show connections. On first meeting the witches we learn that 'fair is foul' (I.1.11), and on first meeting Macbeth he says, 'So foul and fair a day I have not seen' (I.3.39): the echo of 'fair' and 'foul' shows that he is already on their 'wavelength'. Look for other examples that show the influence of witchcraft on the everyday world.

Progress and revision check

REVISION ACTIVITY

❶ Which king did Shakespeare write the play *Macbeth* to please? (Write your answers below)

....

❷ Where (in which country) is the play mostly set?

....

❸ What dominant vice drives Macbeth to commit treason and murder?

....

❹ What themes create the pervading atmosphere of the play?

....

❺ Which characters seek revenge against Macbeth?

....

REVISION ACTIVITY

On a piece of paper write down answers to these questions:

● Discuss Shakespeare's presentation of the theme of ambition in the play and how it affects Macbeth and his wife.

Start: *As soon as the witches speak of Macbeth's future kingship, they touch a nerve inside him; in the same way, when Lady Macbeth reads the letter from her husband she ...*

● How is the theme of witchcraft explored in the play?

Start: *First, witchcraft is important in the play because it dramatically sets the scene: thunder and lightning and the natural order being torn apart ...*

GRADE BOOSTER

Answer this longer, practice question about a theme of the play.

Q: How are supernatural elements and events developed and used in the play?

Think about ...

● The sequence of supernatural elements and events.

● How characters respond to these elements and events, and what that reveals.

For a C grade: explain the elements and events clearly and appropriately and refer to details from the text (use specific examples).

For an A grade: make sure you suggest how the element or event contributes to the meaning of the play and our understanding of the character(s). Focus on developing ideas fully, for example exploring a wide range of connotations from Shakespeare's particular language choices, and the impact they have.

Language

GRADE BOOSTER

Try listening to an audio version of a key speech from the play. Listen to the emphasis that the actor puts on certain words, then try reading the same speech out loud yourself. This can help you to understand and appreciate how Shakespeare's language works.

BLANK VERSE AND KEY IDEAS IN THE PLAY

Blank verse (sometimes called **iambic pentameter**) is the expressive medium in which most of the play is written. The extract below is set out to show where the stresses, or emphases, fall in each line.

I <u>will</u> ad<u>vise</u> you <u>where</u> to <u>plant</u> your<u>selves</u>,
Ac<u>quaint</u> you <u>with</u> the <u>perfect</u> <u>spy</u> o' the <u>time</u>,
The <u>moment</u> <u>on't</u>; for 't <u>must</u> be <u>done</u> to<u>night</u>
And <u>something</u> <u>from</u> the <u>pal</u>ace; <u>always</u> <u>thought</u>
That I require a clearness. And with him
(To leave no rubs, nor botches, in the work),
Fleance his son, that keeps him company,
Whose absence is no less material to me
Than is his father's, must embrace the fate
Of that dark hour. Resolve yourselves apart:
I'll come to you anon. **(III.1.128–38)**

Notice that usually the most important words – nouns/names and verbs/actions – get the emphasis, e.g. plant, spy, done, thought. This gives the key ideas greater prominence. In other words, Shakespeare creates a rhythm which adds another layer of richness to the meanings of the words.

BLANK VERSE AND THE MOODS OF THE CHARACTERS

Blank verse is flexible and its rhythms seem to reflect whatever mood Shakespeare is trying to capture in the **character**.

● being factual and unemotional:

'The Queen, my lord, is dead' **(V.5.16)**

● being argumentative and scoring points:

'Macduff: I have lost my hopes.
Malcolm: Perchance even there, where I did find my doubts' **(IV.3.24–5)**

● being impassioned in a **soliloquy** and calling on demons:

'Come, you spirits / That tend on mortal thoughts, unsex me here!' **(I.5.39–40)**

● being weary, resigned and despairing of life:

'Life's but a walking shadow, a poor player
That struts and frets his hour upon the stage,
And then is heard no more' **(V.5.24–6)**

SHAKESPEARE'S DICTION OR CHOICE OF WORDS

One way that Shakespeare achieves his effects is through his choice of **diction**. A good example of this is:

MACBETH: I have done the deed. – Didst thou not hear a noise?

LADY MACBETH: I heard the owl scream and the crickets cry.
                  Did not you speak?

MACBETH: When?

LADY MACBETH: Now.

MACBETH: As I descended?

LADY MACBETH: Ay.

MACBETH: Hark! Who lies i' the second chamber?

LADY MACBETH: Donalbain.

MACBETH: (*Looking on his hands.*) This is a sorry sight.

Shakespeare here (II.2.14–18) moves away from the grand and poetic language we have seen just earlier with Macbeth – 'Is this a dagger ...' (II.1.33–65). Now Macbeth has committed the murder the language is simple, direct and broken up into a series of short, sharp questions, each one urgent and emotional.

This powerfully reflects the tormented state of mind Macbeth is in, and how he cannot focus on the job in hand. Lady Macbeth, too, is infected by his language, and tries to keep up so that she can get a grip on the situation and control her husband's 'over-reaction' to murder. In studying the play look for unusual words and interesting contrasts of words. Ask, why did Shakespeare choose this word, or this particular contrast?

? DID YOU KNOW

Shakespeare's Insults – Educating your Wit (1991) by Wayne Hill and Cynthia Ottchen is a wonderful compendium of Shakespeare's insults, including those in *Macbeth*.

EXAMINER'S TIP: WRITING ABOUT BLANK VERSE

The flexibility of blank verse is wonderfully demonstrated in Lady Macbeth's reply to her husband's question: 'If we should fail?' (I.7.59). She says, 'We fail?' How many ways can this be said? Spoken flatly, it might suggest what will be, will be. Equally, it might be said in tones of incredulity, or even anxiety. Which is right? Explore how you would say this line, and note what this means for the interpretation of the role.

SHAKESPEARE'S USE OF PROSE

Shakespeare uses **prose** in several scenes, most notably in the letter to Lady Macbeth (I.5), the Porter scene (II.3), the murder of Lady Macduff and her son (IV.2) and the sleep walking of Lady Macbeth (V.1). In each case prose seems entirely appropriate for the task in hand.

The letter to Lady Macbeth is concise yet interesting for what it omits to say. The Porter scene leads to the general observation that Shakespeare frequently used prose when dealing with characters of a lower social standing. Blank verse is more 'noble' or elevated and so more appropriate for nobler characters. Thus, there almost seems a pattern in its use in Macbeth: namely, it does seem to indicate a falling away from nobility or perfection.

KEY CONNECTIONS

There are many tragic figures like Macbeth in literature. Think about Emily Brontë's hero Heathcliff from the novel *Wuthering Heights*. He is passionate but also violent and as the story progresses he becomes increasingly disturbed. Like Macbeth he has an obsession that eventually kills him: rather than ambition, Heathcliff's obsession is his love of Catherine.

Lady Macbeth reads the letter and immediately calls on demons and plans murder. Later, she speaks **prose** when she is mentally disorientated. Lady Macduff begins by speaking in blank verse but as the pressure on her increases prose takes over. She regains the power of **blank verse** – and so dignity – as she confronts the murderers. As for the Porter, his speech is quite overtly obscene as well as being an ordinary person's commentary on the 'hell' (II.3.1) of a place he is in.

SHAKESPEARE'S USE OF VERSE COUPLETS

Verse couplets are used in two important ways. The witches use them in their conversation, and this is entirely appropriate as it suggests the world of spells and incantations. 'Spells' almost always rhyme.

Fillet of a fenny snake,
In the cauldron boil and bake –
Eye of newt, and toe of frog,
Wool of bat and tongue of dog,
Adder's fork, and blind-worms sting,
Lizard's leg, and owlet's wing –
For a charm of powerful trouble,
Like a hell-broth, boil and bubble. (IV.1.12–19)

Frequently, too, Shakespeare has characters conclude a scene with a couplet. This indicates the end of the scene, but also, and often, points to a central idea. For example, Macbeth says that the bell, for Duncan, rings for heaven or hell: 'The bell invites me. / Hear it not, Duncan – for it is a knell / That summons thee to heaven or to hell' (II.1.63–5). The word 'hell' here – rhyming as it does – has extra resonance and depth. Macbeth's action not only produces a heaven or hell consequence for Duncan, it also rings Macbeth's own 'knell'.

WORDS AND THE THEMES OF THE PLAY

Shakespeare uses some words so frequently that they hammer home their importance to the meaning of the play. The repetition creates a dense texture. Words like 'done' (**ironically** the sense of being 'undone' is never far from such 'doing' in the case of Macbeth), 'won', 'lost', 'fair', 'foul'.

If we take just one of these words, 'done', and see a few of its appearances we get some idea of how the word builds up.

- It first appears in Act I: 'When the hurlyburly's done, / When the battle's lost and won' (I.1.3–4)

- Then we meet the word again in the next scene. Ross says, 'I'll see it done' and Duncan replies, ending the scene (see Shakespeare's use of verse couplets), 'What he hath lost, noble Macbeth hath won' (I.ii.69–70)

- Later, Duncan asks, 'Is execution done on Cawdor?' (I.iv.1) and by Scene 5 of the first Act Lady Macbeth is saying: 'That which cries "Thus thou must do" if thou have it – / And that which rather thou dost fear to do, / Than wishest should be undone' (I.v.22–4)

Doing and not-doing – simple ideas and words as they are – clearly relate people to their eternal destiny, as well as the outcomes of this life: winning and losing.

WORDS, IMAGES AND SYMBOLS

The **symbolism** of the play is seamlessly connected with the **imagery**: blood, for example, operates on at least four levels – Donalbain refers to 'near in blood' (II.3.136) as family. It is also what is literally shed when wars and murders occur; it is part of the imagery that pervades the play, creating a sense of menace and destruction; and it is a symbol for the evil that is associated with Macbeth.

It is important in terms of the symbols to remember the Christian and biblical context in which the play was written. Even Macbeth acknowledges heaven and hell, and the references to light and dark. The great Christian symbols – the crucifixion, for example – are not only events from the Bible, but also are symbolic, and they have parallels in *Macbeth*.

We might like to think of Duncan as the innocent and good (Christ-like) king who is betrayed by one of his followers (or disciples), Macbeth. This, of course, parallels Judas Iscariot's betrayal of Christ. As you study the play, you may detect even more parallels – for example, the darkness surrounding the crucifixion, and the darkness on the night of the murder of Duncan.

EXAMINER'S TIP: WRITING ABOUT IMAGERY

Remember to comment on how Shakespeare uses words, sometimes literal, sometimes figurative, to create, through their associations, the rich imagery of the play: blood, dark, light, feasting, clothing and children. Because these words and ideas are constantly being explored and exploited, the effect is to create a wealth of nuances and meanings, ambiguities and insights.

★ GRADE BOOSTER

Where appropriate refer to the language technique used by the writer and the effect it creates. For example, if you say, 'this **metaphor** shows how ...', or 'the effect of this metaphor is to emphasise to the reader ...' this could get you higher marks.

Structure

Macbeth is Shakespeare's shortest **tragedy**. One reason for this is that there is no **subplot**. All the action contributes to the central focus on Macbeth himself. This creates – as befits the intensity of evil in the play – a unified and powerful effect. The play itself has the traditional five Acts, which are then subdivided into scenes. Within that framework the structure is two-fold: we see the rise of Macbeth to power, and we see his fall. Both activities are prefaced by the witches' contributions.

Rise and fall

- In Acts I and II Macbeth rises to a position of power.

- The turning point is in Act III at the banquet scene. Here Macbeth has achieved the full limit and splendour of his power. At this point, Macduff excepted, the thanes of Scotland are prepared to accept him. But the murder of Banquo produces catastrophic consequences, including the immediate taking of Macbeth's chair by the ghost.

- It is following this event that Macbeth decides to revisit the witches, and from here onwards his power declines as his depravity increases.

In this two-fold structure Shakespeare, first, reflects the idea of crime and consequence. Macbeth himself comments on the dangers of 'even-handed justice' (I.7.10) and this proves true in terms of the play's structure: what he does in the first half of the play returns to haunt him in the second half.

Second, Shakespeare shows how the characters of Macbeth and Lady Macbeth pivot round the two-fold structure: it is Lady Macbeth who exults in evil till the middle point of the play, and her husband who is fearful of the damnable consequences; after the assassination of Banquo these positions are reversed.

This point about a two-fold structure should not surprise us when we reflect upon the essential nature of the play: it is about good versus evil, and 'foul' being 'fair' (I.1.11). These oppositions and contrasts run through the whole play.

KEY CONNECTIONS

Try watching the 1997 film version of *Macbeth* starring Jason Connery and Helen Baxendale. Are there any changes that have been made to the structure of the play, e.g. scenes omitted, or events taking place in different order? What effect does this have on the story?

Progress and revision check

REVISION ACTIVITY

❶ What is the form of poetry that most of the play is written in? (Write your answers below)

....

❷ What do we call two lines which rhyme?

....

❸ Why does the Porter speak **prose**?

....

❹ Blood is an image and also a ... what in the play? What does it stand for?

....

❺ Describe the two-fold structure of the play.

....

REVISION ACTIVITY

On a piece of paper write down answers to these questions:

● How does the language they speak show the nature of the characters in Macbeth?

Start: *The nature of the witches and Macbeth is clearly linked by their common vocabulary: they both are preoccupied by what is 'fair' and foul' ...*

● How does the structure of the play help us understand the tragedy of Macbeth?

Start: *Tragedy is about the rise and fall of some great person through some serious weakness they have: we see this exactly represented in Macbeth's rise to power and kingship, culminating in the banquet scene, followed by his depraved decline ...*

GRADE BOOSTER

Answer this longer, practice question about a theme of the play.

Q. How does the language of the play contribute to the atmosphere of evil that Shakespeare creates?

Think about ...

● The diction, imagery and symbols

● The timing – the language shortly before dire events occur.

For a C grade: identify some images and symbols in the text and explain how they are used (give specific examples).

For an A grade: show how the repeated use of a word, image or symbol creates deeper meanings and significance to our understanding of the themes and characters of the play. Explore these meanings and the impact of the language through your own interpretations.

Understanding the question

Questions in examinations or controlled conditions often need **'decoding'**. Decoding the question helps to ensure that your answer will be relevant and refers to what you have been asked.

 UNDERSTAND EXAMINATION LANGUAGE

Get used to examination and essay style language by looking at specimen questions and the words they use. For example:

Exam speak!	Means?	Example
'convey ideas'	*'get across a point to the reader'* Usually you have to say *'how'* this is done.	The arrival of the witches on stage at the start of the play before we see Macbeth could convey the idea that they have conjured him up.
'methods, devices, techniques, ways'	The *'things'* the writer does – such as powerful description, introducing a change of scene, how someone speaks, etc.	Shakespeare might use the technique of drawing parallels between the chaotic world of nature and the fall of Duncan in Act 2 Scene 4.
'present, represent'	1) Present: *'the way things are told to us'* 2) Represent: *'what those things might mean or signify'*.	Shakespeare presents Lady Macbeth sleepwalking and washing her hands in Act 5 Scene 1. This might represent her attempts to wash away her guilt at what she has done.

 'BREAK DOWN' THE QUESTION

Pick out the **key words** or phrases. For example:

Question: How does Shakespeare **convey ideas** about the theme of kingship in the play? Focus on key scenes, such as **Macbeth's soliloquy in Act 1 Scene 7**, and the **dialogue between Macduff and Malcolm in Act 4 Scene 3**.

● The focus is *on* a **theme** – kingship – so this is what you should explore. However, remember to look at what particular **characters** say (**Macbeth, Macduff** and **Malcolm**) which might tell you what you need to know.

● The words **'convey ideas'** mean you need to look at or decide what Shakespeare wanted to say. What makes a good king? Could Macbeth have been a good ruler?

What does this tell you?

● Focus on the theme of kingship (not other themes), and try to interpret or respond to what you think Shakespeare thought about being a king, and what it represented.

KNOW YOUR LITERARY LANGUAGE!

When studying texts you will come across words such as 'theme', 'symbol', 'imagery', 'metaphor' etc. Some of these words could come up in the task or question you are asked. Make sure you know what they mean before you use them!

Planning your answer

t is vital that you **plan** your response to the Controlled Assessment task or possible xam question carefully, and that you then follow your plan, if you are to gain the igher grades.

Do the research!

When revising for the exam, or planning your response to the controlled assessment task, collect **evidence** (for example, quotations) that will support what you have to say. For example, if preparing to answer a question on how Shakespeare has explored the theme of kingship you might list ideas as follows:

Key point	Evidence/quotation	Page/chapter, etc.
Kingship is made up of many qualities. Macbeth may have some, but certainly lacks many, too.	'But I have none: the king-becoming graces, As justice, verity, temperance, stableness, Bounty, perseverance, mercy, lowliness, Devotion, patience, courage, fortitude'	IV.3; when Malcolm is testing Macduff by pretending not to be suitable as a king.

Plan for paragraphs

Use paragraphs to plan your answer. For example:

❶ The first paragraph should **introduce** the **argument** you wish to make.

❷ Then, jot down how the paragraphs that follow will **develop** this argument. Include **details**, **examples** and other possible **points of view**. Each paragraph is likely to deal with one point at a time.

❸ **Sum up** your argument in the last paragraph.

For example, for the following task:

Question: How does Shakespeare present the character of Banquo? Comment on the language devices and techniques used.

Simple plan:

- Paragraph 1: *Introduction*

- Paragraph 2: *First point*, e.g. Banquo returns from battle with Macbeth, enjoying equal status and fame with Macbeth; in fact he is just like Macbeth as a loyal, courageous warrior fighting for his king in battle.

- Paragraph 3: *Second point*, e.g. In the encounter with the witches Banquo's response is very different from Macbeth's: Macbeth's fascination is contrasted with Banquo's warning about the 'instruments of darkness'

- Paragraph 4: *Third point*, e.g. Banquo's integrity is further emphasised when he agrees to speak with Macbeth concerning the three witches, but with the proviso he loses no 'honour'

- Paragraph 5: *Fourth point*, e.g. Banquo's weakness is revealed in his failure to disclose his suspicions following the murder of Duncan.

- Paragraph 6: *Conclusion*

How to use quotations

One of the secrets of success in writing essays is to use quotations **effectively**. There are five basic principles:

❶ Put quotation marks, e.g. ' ' around the quotation.

❷ Write the quotation exactly as it appears in the original.

❸ Do not use a quotation that repeats what you have just written.

❹ Use the quotation so that it fits into your sentence or if it is longer, indent it as a separate paragraph.

❺ Only quote what is most useful.

EXAMINER'S TIP

Try using a quotation to begin your response. You can use it as a launch-pad for your ideas, or as an idea you are going to argue against.

TOP TIP ✓ **USE QUOTATIONS TO DEVELOP YOUR ARGUMENT**

Quotations should be used to develop the line of thought in your essays. Your comment should not duplicate what is in your quotation. For example:

GRADE D/E   GRADE C

(simply repeats the idea)	(makes a point and supports it with a relevant quotation)
Duncan thinks that you cannot read a person's mind from looking at their face, 'There's no art / To find the mind's construction in the face'	Duncan seems to understand how difficult it is to judge people when he says, 'There's no art / To find the mind's construction in the face'

However the most sophisticated way of using the writer's words is to embed them into your sentence, and further develop the point:

GRADE A

(makes point, embeds quote and develops idea)
Duncan seems to understand human nature when he comments on the impossibility of finding the 'mind's construction in the face', but this does not prevent him being fooled a second time by the scheming of Macbeth and his wife. Nor does he spot how other superficial things, such as the 'pleasant seat' of Macbeth's castle, might hide their murderous intentions.

When you use quotations in this way, you are demonstrating the ability to use text as evidence to support your ideas – not simply including words from the original to prove you have read it.

Sitting the examination

Examination papers are carefully designed to give you the opportunity to do your best. Follow these handy hints for examination success:

BEFORE YOU START

- Make sure that you **know the texts** you are writing about so that you are properly prepared and equipped.

- You need to be **comfortable** and **free from distractions**. Inform the invigilator if anything is off-putting, e.g. a shaky desk.

- **Read** and follow the instructions, or rubric, on the front of the examination paper. You should know by now what you need to do but **check** to reassure yourself.

- Before beginning your answer have a **skim** through the **whole paper** to make sure you don't miss anything **important**.

- Observe the **time allocation** – and follow it carefully. If they recommend 45 minutes for a particular question on a text make sure this is how long you spend.

WRITING YOUR RESPONSES

A typical 45 minute examination essay is probably between 550 and 800 words in length.

Ideally, spend a minimum of 5 minutes planning your answer before you begin.

Use the questions to structure your response. Here is an example:

Question: Do you see the ending of the play as negative or positive? What methods does the writer use to lead you to this view?

- The introduction to your answer could briefly describe **the ending** of the novel;

- the second part could explain what could be seen as **positive**;

- the third part could be an exploration of the **negative** aspects;

- the conclusion would **sum up your own viewpoint**.

For each part allocate paragraphs to cover the points you wish to make (see **Planning your answer**).

Keep your writing clear and easy to read, using paragraphs and link words to show the structure of your answers.

Spend a couple of minutes afterwards quickly checking for obvious errors.

'KEY WORDS' ARE THE KEY!

Keep on mentioning the **key words** from the question in your answer. This will keep you on track AND remind the examiner that you are answering the question set.

★ GRADE BOOSTER

Stick to a standard essay format. Your beginning should outline where your essay is going, not repeat the question; your middle should comprise the main facts, avoiding generalisations; and your ending should summarise the main points in a logical and coherent manner. Remember, most marks are for the 'middle' bit.

Sitting the controlled assessment

It may be the case that you are responding to *Macbeth* in a controlled assessment situation. Follow these useful tips for success.

 **WHAT YOU ARE REQUIRED TO DO**

Make sure you are clear about:

- The **specific text** and **task** you are preparing (is it just *Macbeth*, or more than one play/text?)
- How **long** you have during the assessment period (i.e. 3–4 hours)?
- How **much** you are expected or allowed to write (i.e. 2,000 words)?
- **What** you are **allowed to take** into the controlled assessment, and what you can use (or not, as the case may be!) You may be able to take in brief notes but **not** draft answers, so check with your teacher.

★ **GRADE BOOSTER**

Make sure your handwriting is clear and legible: it makes it much easier for examiners and markers to give you the grade you deserve. To do this, space out your writing, and ensure that no two letters look exactly the same. If word-processing, use the spell check and make sure you space your text.

TOP TIP **HOW YOU CAN PREPARE**

Once you know your task, topic and text/s you can:

- Make **notes** and **prepare** the **points, evidence, quotations**, etc. you are likely to use.
- Practise or draft **model answers**.
- Use these **York Notes** to hone your **skills**, e.g. use of quotations, how to plan an answer and focus on what makes a **top grade.**

TOP TIP **DURING THE CONTROLLED ASSESSMENT**

Remember:

- **Stick** to the topic and task you have been given.
- The allocated **time** is for **writing,** so make the most of it. It is double the time you might have in an examination, so you will be writing almost **twice as much** (or more).
- **If** you are **allowed** access to a **dictionary or thesaurus** make use of them; if not, don't go near them!
- At the end of the controlled assessment follow your **teacher's instructions.** For example, make sure you have written your **name** clearly on all the pages you hand in.

Improve your grade

t is useful to know the type of responses examiners are looking for when they award different grades. The following broad guidance should help you to improve your grade when responding to the task you are set!

GRADE C

What you need to show	What this means
Sustained response to task and text	You write enough! You don't run out of ideas after two paragraphs.
Effective use of **details** to **support your explanations**	You generally support what you say with evidence, e.g. there are clues that Lady Macbeth may not be as strong as she appears when she says she couldn't kill Duncan as he 'resembled my father as he slept' [Act 2 Scene 2]
Explanation of the writer's **use of language, structure, form**, etc., and the **effect on readers**	You must write about the writer's use of these things. It's not enough simply to give a viewpoint. So, you might comment on how **contrasts** are used by Shakespeare to convey ideas about good and evil, such as Macbeth's very first words in the play – 'foul and fair' – to describe the day in Act 1 Scene 3.
Appropriate comment on **characters, plot, themes, ideas** and **settings**	What you say is relevant. If the task asks you to comment on how Banquo is presented, that is who you write about.

GRADE A

What you need to show *in addition* to the above	What this means
Insightful, exploratory response to the text	You look beyond the obvious. You might question the idea of Banquo's goodness – where might his ambition have led if he hadn't been killed?
Close analysis and use of detail	If you are looking at Shakespeare's use of language, you comment on each word in a line or phrase drawing out its distinctive effect on the reader, e.g. when Macbeth praises [and fears] Banquo's 'royalty of nature' the word, 'royalty' both compares him to a king, and reminds us why Macbeth needs to kill him.
Convincing and **imaginative interpretation**	Your viewpoint is likely to convince the examiner. You show you have *engaged* with the text, and come up with your own ideas. These may be based on what you have discussed in class or read about, but you have made your own decisions.

Annotated sample answers

This section will provide you with **extracts** from **two** model answers, one at **C grade** and one at **A grade**, to give you an idea of what is required to achieve at different levels.

> **Question:** Read from Act 1 Scene 7 ('If it were done when 'tis done, then 'twere well ... False face must hide what the false heart doth know.') Answer both parts of the question:
>
> A How does Macbeth's opening soliloquy contribute to our understanding of his character?
>
> B How does Shakespeare convey Lady Macbeth's influence over her husband in the scene and through the play?

CANDIDATE 1

Good quotation to use to indicate the moral dilemma

When the scene opens Shakespeare presents Macbeth trying to decide whether he is going to kill king Duncan or not. The first line says, 'If it were done when 'tis done, then 'twere well It were done quickly'. This means that if he decides to kill Duncan, then he needs to do it quickly. But he then argues, even if he does the deed quickly, there is the problem of the consequences of the murder: 'we but teach / Bloody instructions, which, being taught, return / To plague the inventor'. Macbeth is worried that if he does evil, it will return upon him.

What does this say about character?

Shows Macbeth's imagination well

We see in this his quick mind, as he lists the facts, and also his vivid imagination as he pictures some of the possible consequences, like when he uses the image of a child: 'And pity, like a naked new-born babe'. At the same time, all the arguments against doing it come down to his final comment about his 'vaulting ambition'. The passage shows a man of imagination, insight, and moral standards, but also one who is too ambitious.

Fair summary of his character qualities

Right to move to second part of the question

Lady Macbeth arrives just at the right moment: as Macbeth seems ready to 'proceed no further', she challenges his decision. She is more ambitious at the start than her husband. And here she uses her key argument on him that she uses later: 'Art thou afeard / To be the same in thine own act and valour / As thou art in desire?' What this means is: are you really a man, do you have the courage of a man? Later when the murder has been committed, Lady Macbeth criticises Macbeth for being frightened to go back and smear the guards with blood. She has to do it.

No supporting quotation here

Weak statement

Shakespeare shows us that Lady Macbeth has a big influence on her husband. So far as encouraging him to commit murder, she is very successful. Later, however, she becomes less successful in influencing him. She recognises that he needs 'sleep' in order to recover his powers, but instead he decides to visit the witches. From then on she has little or no influence on him.

Good example, not often used

Overall comment: This is a solid essay in which the student supports his/her views with some well chosen quotations. Occasionally the points are not supported by evidence, and while the answer is clear and well argued there is little evidence of original thinking or a developed personal response. Perhaps more reference to Lady Macbeth's language in influencing Macbeth would help here.

GRADE C

CANDIDATE 2

Excellent selection of one word and its full impact

The witches have already activated the lurking ambition inside Macbeth; now Shakespeare organises events which conspire to bring Duncan within his grasp. Macbeth is shown wrestling with his scruples, 'If it were done' – the key word is, 'If'. If he could do it, get away with it, he reasons, then he should do it. But he knows, at a deep level, 'we still have judgement here'. All the arguments for doing it are slight compared with Shakespeare's extraordinary figurative language in the pleading images of 'angels', 'Pity' personified, and the hyperbole of 'every eye' that will witness what he has done. Yet, 'vaulting ambition' may drive him on – vaulting being a powerful, athletic metaphor, suggesting leaping over all obstacles.

Powerful alignment of brief quotations and analysis of figures of speech

Shakespeare, therefore, conveys to us a character determined and ambitious, yet sensitive, imaginative – poetic even – not wanting to give in to his evil side, but also profoundly restless: the torrent of words will not really allow him to listen to his own conscience. He argues he should not do the deed just at the very point his wife appears: perhaps he knows she will persuade him otherwise. Shakespeare has earlier used the image of that 'milk of human kindness' to express what Lady Macbeth feels about her husband's good nature, and how she needs to empty it from him. So, he is right to be worried.

Original observation about the torrent of words

Controversial idea but good use of supporting text outside the scene

And her influence is profound. Before this scene, she too has been in touch with supernatural forces, saying, 'unsex me here', which dehumanise her. Macbeth himself says, 'Bring forth men-children only' in recognition of this fact. The point is, Shakespeare shows Macbeth is fascinated by the witches, and now Lady Macbeth becomes their human instrument. Perhaps as she has become figuratively a 'man', now Macbeth has to become 'more' than a man. He says himself, 'who dares do more, is none', but to no avail. Courage is confused with daring to do a wicked deed. On this one argument Lady Macbeth influences him to murder his kinsman, guest and king.

Smooth transition to second part of question and link to earlier scenes

Well developed point

Neat summary

After the murder, Shakespeare shows her influence in decline. Macbeth is made strong by 'hard use'; Lady Macbeth is kept out of the murderous loop, and her husband's confidence. As he initiates a reign of terror, she retires to her room, sleep walking, and destined to commit a lonely suicide.

Some good points, but feels rushed and ends without supporting evidence

Overall comment: This is an outstanding response with few weak points. Quotations and evidence are woven skilfully into the answer, and there are several examples of original thinking and ideas. The final paragraph is slightly weaker, and would benefit from considering Lady Macbeth's role in the banquet scene. Overall, however, this is very successful.

GRADE A

Further questions

❶ Choose a scene from *Macbeth* which you think is a turning point. Write about this scene, bringing out its importance in the play as a whole.

❷ Write about a major theme of the play *Macbeth*.

❸ Write about the impact the character of Lady Macbeth has on the reader/ audience.

❹ Write about Shakespeare's use of imagery in *Macbeth* with particular reference to two or three major images.

❺ Outline Macbeth's involvement with the witches. To what extent are they responsible for what happens in the play?

❻ A How does Shakespeare show Macbeth's thoughts and feelings in I.4: 'The Prince of Cumberland: that is a step ...'

   B Explain how Shakespeare shows Macbeth having different thoughts and feelings in a scene later in the play.

❼ A How does Shakespeare make the dialogue between Macbeth and Lady Macbeth dramatic and tense in I.7: 'How now, what news? ...'?

   B Show how Shakespeare uses dialogue to create a dramatic and tense moment in another part of the play.

❽ A How does the extract from the scene II.3: 'O, horror, horror, horror ...' sustain an audience's interest and affect its feelings about any **two** of the characters in it?

   B How does Shakespeare show Macduff or Lady Macbeth in a different way at another point in the play?

❾ A How does Shakespeare present the feelings and the relationship between Malcolm and Macduff in IV.3: 'Let us seek out some desolate ...'?

   B How does Shakespeare portray different aspects of Malcolm and Macduff's relationship, character and mood at another point in the play?

❿ A What does I.1 contribute to the plot and the themes of the play?

   B Explain how Shakespeare develops the plot and theme of this scene in another scene later in the play.

LITERARY TERMS

Literary term	Explanation
blank verse	unrhymed
character(s)	either a person in a play, novel, etc. or his or her personality
couplet	a pair of rhymed lines of any metre – so verse couplet
diction	the choice of words in a work of fiction; the kind of vocabulary used
doggerel	bad verse – ill-constructed, rough, clumsy versification
dramatic irony	when the development of the plot allows the audience to possess more information about what is happening than some of the characters themselves have
figurative	any form of expression which deviates from the plainest expression of meaning
foreshadow	a warning of something that will follow later
hyperbole	emphasis by exaggeration
iambic	consisting of the iamb – which is the commonest metrical foot in English verse. It has two syllables, consisting of one weak stress followed by a strong stress, ti-*tum*
iambic pentameter	a line of five iambs
imagery	its narrowest meaning is a word-picture. More commonly, imagery refers to figurative language in which words that refer to objects and qualities appeal to the senses and the feelings. Often imagery is expressed through metaphor
irony	saying one thing when another is meant
metaphor	a comparison in which one thing is said (or implied) to be another
motif	some aspect of literature (a type of character, theme or image) which recurs frequently
pathos	moments in a work of art which evoke strong feelings of pity and sorrow
pentameter	in versification a line of five feet – often iambic
personification	a metaphor in which things or ideas are treated as if they were human beings, with human attributes and feelings
prose	any language that is not made patterned by the regularity of metre
simile	a comparison in which one thing is said to be 'like' or 'as' another
soliloquy	a dramatic convention allowing a character to speak directly to the audience, as if thinking aloud his or her thoughts and feelings
subplot	a story containing minor characters in a play
symbol	something which represents something else, e.g. a rose standing for beauty
theme	the central idea or ideas that the play is about
tragedy	a story that traces the career and downfall of an individual and shows in this downfall both the capacities and limitations of human life
verse	poetry, usually with a regular metrical pattern
vocabulary	the choice of words a writer uses

CHECKPOINT ANSWERS

- By asking questions and riddles
- By referring to elemental forces
- By their appearance

CHECKPOINT 2

Because they are saying exactly what he wants to hear and this can only be because they touch a nerve already present in Macbeth.

CHECKPOINT 3

If Macbeth is to be king, then this is something or someone he must overcome. It appears to trigger in Macbeth a deeper level of plotting and treason.

CHECKPOINT 4

This is a theme running through the play. Other examples include:

- Lady Macbeth greeting Duncan (I.6)
- Macbeth on learning of Duncan's murder (II.3)
- Macbeth enquiring about Banquo's ride (III.1)
- Macbeth at the banquet for Banquo (III.4)

CHECKPOINT 5

His openness is in admitting his feelings – which is in stark contrast to Macbeth, who flatly lies that he doesn't think about the witches.

CHECKPOINT 6

To prevent discussion of what actually did happen that night. To prevent the guards denying their involvement in Duncan's murder.

CHECKPOINT 7

Vitally important, despite only appearing in a handful of scenes. Macbeth himself is aware of just how bad he is by contrast with Duncan. Duncan is a touchstone for true kingship and a measure of how a king should be. Set against his standard, Macbeth falls miserably short.

CHECKPOINT 8

Macbeth's character is degrading as he swims deeper in evil; he no longer really trusts – or cares about – anybody. As he says in III.4.135–6: 'For mine own good, / All causes shall give way'.

CHECKPOINT 9

Up till then they may have been prepared to accept Macbeth in the interests of peace, and simply to give him the benefit of the doubt. Now they know they must – and do – act.

CHECKPOINT 10

The quest for total security is impossible, and in seeking it Macbeth ironically achieves exactly the opposite: for example, Banquo is a threat, but in murdering Banquo most of the other thanes turn against him, thus creating more danger, and less security.

CHECKPOINT 11

The sense of evil is heightened by: sounds – thunder, music and incantations – as well as sights: the witches, their masters and the apparitions themselves. Macbeth's own dramatic and wicked intentions only add to the sense of urgency of the evil.

CHECKPOINT 12

He is testing Macduff's integrity because – with all the spies and traitors that Macbeth has created – he is afraid that Macduff might be on Macbeth's side.

CHECKPOINT 13

Ironically, by his obsessive and literal belief in them. Believing the Wood to be moving, he thinks the prophecy has come true and that he is, therefore, doomed. Because of this, instead of staying in his castle that would 'laugh a seige to scorn' (line 3), he rides out to battle – even though he knows he does not have enough troops to win. Thus, he ensures the prophecy comes true.